Lauren closed her eyes. "Don't do this to me," she pleaded softly to the man called Greg.

He noticed that she never used his name when she was talking to him. She avoided calling him either Jon or Greg, no doubt trying to keep her emotional distance from him. "Don't do what?"

"Call up feelings and memories from the past. I can't deal with them.... I'm not sure who you are.... I'll help you, but leave the past buried."

Her words were a challenge, and he wanted to push her into admitting he was Jon, her husband. But what he wanted most was to lose himself in her heat.

"All right," he answered. "I'll agree to not bring up the past. But be warned, when this is over and you're safe again, I intend to pursue my claim."

Dear Reader,

We've got some great reading for you this month, but I'll bet you already knew that. Suzanne Carey is back with *Whose Baby?* The title already tells you that a custody battle is at the heart of this story, but it's Suzanne's name that guarantees all the emotional intensity you want to find between the covers.

Maggie Shayne's *The Littlest Cowboy* launches a new miniseries this month, THE TEXAS BRAND. These rough, tough, ranchin' Texans will win your heart, just as Sheriff Garrett Brand wins the hearts of lovely Chelsea Brennan and her tiny nephew. If you like mysterious and somewhat spooky goings-on, you'll love Marcia Evanick's *His Chosen Bride*, a marriage-of-convenience story with a paranormal twist. Clara Wimberly's hero in *You Must Remember This* is a mysterious stranger—mysterious even to himself, because his memory is gone and he has no idea who he is or what has brought him to Sarah James's door. One thing's for certain, though: it's love that keeps him there. In *Undercover Husband*, Leann Harris creates a heroine who thinks she's a widow, then finds out she might not be when a handsome—and somehow familiar—stranger walks through her door. Finally, I know you'll love *Prince Joe*, the hero of Suzanne Brockmann's new book, part of her TALL, DARK AND DANGEROUS miniseries. This is a royal impostor story, with a rough-around-the-edges hero who suddenly has to wear the crown.

Don't miss a single one of these exciting books, and come back next month for more of the best romance around—only in Silhouette Intimate Moments.

Yours,

Leslie Wainger
Senior Editor and Editorial Coordinator

Please address questions and book requests to:
Silhouette Reader Service
U.S.: 3010 Walden Ave., P.O. Box 1325, Buffalo, NY 14269
Canadian: P.O. Box 609, Fort Erie, Ont. L2A 5X3

UNDERCOVER HUSBAND

LEANN HARRIS

Published by Silhouette Books

America's Publisher of Contemporary Romance

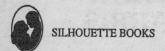

SILHOUETTE BOOKS

ISBN 0-373-07719-X

UNDERCOVER HUSBAND

Books by Leann Harris

Silhouette Intimate Moments

Bride on the Run #516
Angel at Risk #618
Trouble in Texas #664
Undercover Husband #719

LEANN HARRIS

When Leann Harris first met her husband in college, she never dreamed she would marry him. After all, he was getting a Ph.D. in the one science she'd managed to avoid—physics! So much for first impressions. They have been happily married for over twenty years. After graduating from the University of Texas at Austin, Leann taught math and science to deaf high school students until the birth of her first child. It wasn't until her youngest child started school that Leann decided to fulfill a lifelong dream, and began writing. She presently lives in Plano, Texas, with her husband and two children.

ACKNOWLEDGMENTS

I would like to thank the following people for their
help on this book:

Linda Deleon-Campbell, who cheerfully answered all
my questions on embassies and the Department of State,
and went out of her way to help me.

Lt. Dave Davis of the Dallas Police Department,
who is always a lifesaver in plotting and police matters.
Thank you for getting me out of my tight spot.

Chapter 1

The envelope looked innocent. Plain. White. In the top right corner, Elizabeth II smiled regally. The cancellation stamp read London. Below, "Lauren Michaels" was neatly typed.

After closing the door to her apartment, Lauren turned the envelope over, ripped it open and pulled out the single sheet of paper.

"How Tall Is Red?"

The familiar surroundings of the living room faded as she stared at the note, which was written in a distinctive script that was a unique combination of cursive and printed letters.

The rest of her mail slipped through her numb fingers, falling to the floor.

Cass, her neighbor from across the hall, glanced up from the dining room table. "Are you all right?" she asked.

Quickly Lauren stuffed the note in her skirt pocket and bent to retrieve the scattered envelopes. "Yes."

"You're so pale. If I didn't know better, I'd swear you'd seen a ghost."

Cassie wasn't far off the mark. Lauren threw the remaining mail on a wingback chair, then joined her friend at the table. Tonight they were to finish addressing invitations to Lauren's bridal shower.

Although Cass chatted about the plans for the shower, Lauren couldn't concentrate on a thing said. The paper in her pocket was burning a hole through her skirt.

Four words. Twelve letters. Not much of a note by anyone's standards, except she didn't know any ghosts who jotted messages and mailed them by the Royal Mail.

When Cass left an hour and a half later, Lauren breathed an audible sigh of relief.

"I quite agree. I thought she would never leave."

Lauren whirled in her chair and gasped at the sight of the tall man who stood inside the open French doors. The upper half of his body was hidden by the shadows. His legs, encased in tan slacks, were in the light. Her heart stopped as if a cold steel hand squeezed her chest, and the fear racing through her veins held her immobile.

"It's very careless of you to leave your patio doors open," the man commented casually. "Anyone could get in."

Lauren tried to speak, but her tongue seemed glued to the roof of her mouth. She swallowed to moisten the dry interior, then said, "Who are you?"

The intruder stepped forward, and it was then that she noticed the cane in his right hand. He did not lean heavily upon it, but his slight limp was evident.

"I'm the one who sent the letter." His accent told her he was American, like her. His voice was deep and gravelly, as if something terrible had happened to it. He settled himself in the chair Cass had recently occupied.

Staring wide-eyed, Lauren took in every detail of the man's appearance, from his mane of black hair to his brown eyes to the close-clipped salt-and-pepper beard and mustache. It was a handsome face, but not one she knew.

"That's impossible."

"Why?"

"Because my husband wrote that note, and he's dead."

There was a long pause. Then he said, "Do you often receive mail from dead people?"

Lauren leapt to her feet, her chair skidding backward. Anger eclipsed her fear. "Who are you and what do you want?"

"I am the one who wrote that note," he calmly repeated. "I'm Jonathan Michaels."

"Stop it!"

He leaned forward. "Would you like for me to tell you what the note says?"

Raising her chin, she accepted his challenge. "Yes, tell me."

"How tall is red?"

She fumbled for the chair behind her. If she didn't sit down immediately, she'd fall flat on her behind.

"That's the title of the mystery you always wanted to write. You and I thought it up one afternoon on our honeymoon, when we were on the beach in Ayr."

Lauren felt as if she'd just gotten off the Tilt-A-Whirl at the state fair, disoriented, confused and sick to her stomach. "That's not possible."

"We rented a little cottage about a half mile from the beach," he continued.

"We?" she whispered.

"Don't you remember? On a clear day, we could see Northern Ireland. You loved Ayr, wanted to rent a cottage for the summer and write your novel. Only we never got a chance."

Carefully she studied the man before her who claimed to be Jon. His slim nose and sensuous lips, framed by his beard and mustache, combined to make a very handsome man in spite of the thin scar that ran from his left temple into his beard.

"If you expect me to believe a lie that big, you should at least have brown hair and blue eyes like Jon had."

He ran his fingers through the black thickness, ruffling it and causing several strands to fall onto his forehead. "The hair's dyed, and I've got colored contacts to hide my true identity."

"Prove it," she demanded.

Without a moment's hesitation, he took out the right contact. His eye was blue.

"Take out the other."

He shrugged, put in the contact on his finger and took out the other. Blue again. Her stomach knotted into a tight ball.

"Satisfied?" he asked, replacing the second contact.

"No," she said, fighting against confusion tugging at her reason. "Lots of people have blue eyes."

"You're being your usual stubborn self, Lauren."

He said her name in an intimate tone that made her think of dark nights and heated passion. It was too much for her to bear. "This is absurd. You're not Jonathan Michaels, and if you're not out of here in thirty seconds, I'm going to call the cops."

His hand covered hers. The movement startled her, but his hold was gentle. And spine tingling. That was the thing that had first drawn her to Jon, the fiery chemistry between them.

"Give me five minutes. If I can't explain everything to your satisfaction, then I'll leave with no trouble."

She wanted to deny his request, but he seemed to know too many things that no one besides Jon would know. She needed to hear his explanation or be forever haunted. "All right. You have five minutes." She glanced at her watch.

His mouth curved in a smile that drew Lauren's attention to his lips. "I always did like your no-nonsense ways."

Lauren pushed aside the awareness and said, "You now have four minutes and thirty-nine seconds."

He rubbed his hand over his chin and mouth, then fingered the thin scar by his left ear. "What did the embassy tell you when they informed you of my death?"

"What does that have to do with anything?"

"It's important, Lauren, what you know of the circumstances surrounding my alleged death."

"I was told the brakes on my husband's car failed as he was driving through the Alps. What I still don't understand is why he was in France when he was supposed to be building a hotel in Belgium."

The man shook his head. "I was on my way to meet a Czech embassy officer who was going to tell me the identity of a mole who had compromised several key NATO installations and projects. Only I never made the rendezvous because someone tampered with the brakes of my car.''

''What were you—I mean, what was Jon doing meeting that man?''

He shook his head at her refusal to acknowledge him as Jon. ''Because, Lauren, that's what I do. It's what I was and am. A spy.''

All this talk of spies and espionage was preposterous. Things like this only happened in James Bond movies, not to an east Texas girl who owned a Mexican restaurant in London a block from the American embassy. ''I don't believe you. If Jon had been a spy, I would've known. He was a structural engineer who oversaw the building of hotels for American companies in Europe.''

''A cover. The job provided a nice cover, especially in Eastern Europe. My real assignment was counterintelligence. Europe was my speciality. That's why I was based out of London.''

''I don't believe you. Since the Communist regimes fell, all this spy business is rather out of vogue, wouldn't you say?''

His harsh laughter bounced off the walls. ''What do you think all those Communist spies did once their paychecks stopped?''

She bit her bottom lip. ''I don't know. Stopped spying?''

''That's one of the qualities I loved the most about you. Your ability to always hope for the best.'' He ran his fingers through his hair and sighed. ''No, sweet, those individuals didn't give up the spying game. They simply found new employers or they went independent and started selling to the highest bidder, the North Koreans, the Chinese, international terrorist organizations." His hands knotted into fists. "Anyone with enough cash can buy any secret or weapon they want. We're in worse shape now than before. When the wall fell in Berlin, the guys in the Stasi—the East German secret service—just up and disappeared, and I shudder to think what they are doing now."

The picture he painted was bleak and something she didn't want to deal with at this moment. "Okay, I'll admit you have a point. But what does that have to do with me?"

He smiled sadly. "Nothing. It has nothing to do with you."

"Then why are you here, claiming to be Jon? For heaven's sake, you don't even look like my husband."

He leaned back in the chair. "My injuries from the accident were extensive. I went through the windshield of the car, but luckily I was thrown clear of the explosion and fire." Absently he rubbed his right thigh. "My face was messed up and vocal cords damaged. Both my legs and arms were broken in multiple places. After three years of physical therapy, I was well enough to return to London."

"If that's true, then why didn't the hospital contact me? Why send me an urn with ashes? And why, after all this time, have you decided to show up now?"

"Since I didn't discover the identity of the mole, and the Czech I was to meet died in a nasty accident, my superior and I decided that, for my protection and yours, he would float the story I'd been killed. After I recovered enough, my boss assigned me back to the London station to try to catch this mole. I was introduced as Greg Williams, and I've been working quietly here in London for the last six months. Nobody at the embassy knows my true identity."

Anger washed through her. "Six months? You've been here six months and haven't tried to contact me before now?"

"So you do believe I'm Jonathan, your husband."

"No," she snapped, annoyed with herself for momentarily believing his lies.

His gaze held hers, and rivers of fire danced up and down her spine. "I stayed away for your safety. If the mole knew I was alive, he might use you to get to me. The reason I'm here now is because there was a break-in in the embassy a couple of weeks ago. In the course of the investigation, some of the fingerprints lifted were ones belonging to Jonathan Michaels. My superior has tried to keep the information as classified as possible. But the mole may know I'm alive. Only, if he does, he doesn't know under what cover name I'm operating. I came to warn you to be careful. You might be in danger."

Lauren felt as if she were being ripped apart inside. *If* what this man said was true . . . No. That reality was too painful to contemplate after years of pain and longing for Jon. Suddenly Lauren's temper flared at the atrocious untruths this man was feeding her. Welcoming the strong emotion because it provided a shield for her wounded heart, she snapped, "I haven't heard such an awful lie since my mother's third husband told her he wasn't fooling around. Your story stinks, mister. If— and I stress the word *if*—Jonathan was a spy, why would he marry a simple girl from Kaufman, Texas? I know nothing of spies and lying."

His deep, rich laugh sent a chill down her spine.

"You were never a simple country girl. Shrewd, resourceful, smart but never simple. And you were honest, something I hadn't seen in a very long time. You were water to my thirsty soul, Lauren. Loving you made me whole again.''

She took a deep, slow breath, trying to regain control of her ragged emotions. "You're good with words.''

"You liked that about me. You said I should have been a writer instead of an engineer.''

A sound, somewhere between a sob and cry, caught in her throat. The man stood, walked around the corner of the table and pulled Lauren to her feet. When he tried to embrace her, she slapped away his hands. "Don't.''

He sighed, deeply, sadly. "I didn't come back to torment you, sweetheart. I came to warn you.'' He picked up one of the open invitations on the table, examined it, then set it down. "I saw your wedding announcement in the paper. We're still married.''

"Jonathan Michaels is legally dead.''

"Maybe in the eyes of the law. But that doesn't change the fact that I'm still alive. I still consider myself married to you.''

Her chin jerked up, and tears gathered in her eyes. She tried to blink back the moisture, but a single tear ran down her cheek.

He brushed his thumb across her cheek, wiping away the wetness. "When I saw the announcement, everything in me rebelled. I threw my coffee mug against the wall of my kitchen.'' He shook his head. "That's a bad sign for a spy, Lauren. Emotional attachments are something we can't afford. They can be used against us. That's why I stayed away.''

Embarrassed by her reaction, she swiped the rest of the moisture from her cheeks.

His eyes were shadowed, as if he were haunted by some dark tragedy. "It was the thought of coming back to you, Lauren, that helped me survive three years ago. My heart wouldn't let go." His finger lightly traced her jaw. "How can I prove to you I'm Jonathan Michaels, your husband?"

Her mind raced. Did Jon have any distinguishing marks? "When Jon was eight he was caught in a barbed-wire fence. The scar was on..." Her cheeks burned with embarrassment.

Her tormentor's lips curved into a broad grin. "Yes. Where's the scar?"

"If you're who you claim you are, you'll know where the scar is," she answered indignantly.

She tried to outstare him, but when his hands went to his belt buckle, her eyes dropped to the floor. As she listened to the rustle of fabric and the sound of his zipper, the color in her face went two shades brighter. Why couldn't she have thought of another distinguishing mark?

"Lauren."

Her head jerked up, and she glued her eyes to his face.

"Unless you look lower, you'll never know if there's a scar on my thigh or not."

Her eyes moved quickly down his body, trying to ignore the wide shoulders and deep chest. Thankfully his shirt covered his briefs. When her eyes settled on his thighs, she went still. His legs were covered with a dozen scars. Some were thin, straight lines. Others were jagged. His right knee was surrounded by angry red lines, sure signs of trauma. The spot where Jon's scar should have been was covered with a gigantic red scar.

"What happened?"

"The car accident. My legs were cut by flying glass and broken in seven places."

She continued to gape until he cleared his throat and pulled up his trousers. She flushed again.

"Why didn't you just tell me you had all those scars on your legs, instead of dropping your pants?" she demanded indignantly.

"Would you have believed me if I simply told you?"

"No." She hadn't felt like such a prize fool since she was eight and stepped in a cow patty in front of the entire third grade when they'd gone on a field trip to a local dairy.

"Is there anything else you want me to remove?"

She glared at him. "Don't be smart. I've never appreciated that trait in men."

"Does your fiancé have traits you appreciate?"

She caught the slight edge of bitterness in his tone.

"You need more proof, don't you, Lauren?" He didn't wait for an answer but sat at the table. The man hooked his cane over the edge of the table and, with his right hand, picked up the pen she'd used to address invitations. Ah-hah, Lauren thought triumphantly to herself. She'd caught the impostor. At that moment he glanced up, flashed her a devilish grin, then transferred the pen to his left hand.

Lauren watched in growing horror as he turned over the shower list and wrote his name in the unique style of printed letters and cursive that was her husband's. When he finished, he pushed the paper toward Lauren.

"It's easy to forge a signature."

He didn't say anything but wrote her entire name, Lauren Mary Crocker Michaels, then listed her date and place of birth and the names of her parents.

"It's not true," she mumbled to herself, feeling sick.

The doorbell rang, startling them.

"Lauren," came Cass's muffled voice from the hall.

"Don't tell anyone I've been here," the man claiming to be Jon whispered in Lauren's ear.

"Lauren," Cass called again.

"Just a minute," Lauren answered. Standing, she started toward the door, but the stranger's hand on her arm stopped her.

"Remember, not a word to anyone. Your life and mine depend on your silence."

Before Lauren could take another step, the doorknob turned and Cass hurried into the apartment. Lauren panicked. Cass was the biggest gossip in the building, and within a half hour every one of their friends would know that Lauren Michaels was entertaining a strange man in her flat.

"I just came back for my glasses," she said, scurrying toward the dining table. "I don't want to miss a single moment of the soccer game."

Lauren braced herself for Cass's screech, but nothing happened.

"Thanks, luv," Cass said over her shoulder as she rushed by Lauren, holding her glasses high. At the door, she paused. "Are you feeling under the weather? You look pale."

Lauren shook her head.

Cass smiled. "I'll call tomorrow."

Dumbfounded, Lauren turned. The room was empty. She walked slowly through her apartment, looking for the mystery man. He'd vanished. Probably through the open French doors not three feet from the table.

Lauren reached in her pocket and withdrew the crumpled letter. With shaking fingers she put it on the dining room table and smoothed out the wrinkles. The penned words jumped out at her.

Her knees weakened and she collapsed into a chair. It couldn't be true. Jon couldn't be alive. She covered her face with her hands and took a deep breath. The grief over Jon's death had nearly killed her. It had only been during the past eighteen months that she felt like a whole person again, and her recent decision to remarry had been a hard-fought battle with her heart.

And yet this strange man had known about the mystery she wanted to write, the facts of her birth, and his handwriting was a dead ringer for Jon's. Even the chemistry between them felt right.

"It can't be," she whispered. "It just can't be." Even as she denied the possibility, her heart leapt at the prospect.

"Did she believe you? Buy your story?" Diamond asked from the other end of the phone line.

"I don't know."

"You mean you couldn't convince her?"

"The lady's no fool. And you'll have to admit my story sounds rather farfetched." The man readjusted the phone to his ear as he stared out the window. "I don't think she knows what to think. Only time will tell. I'll let you know how things progress."

But time wasn't a commodity he had, he thought ruefully. He had the ugly suspicion that the game had begun, even if all the players weren't in place.

Moments later Diamond hung up the phone, then leaned back in his chair. He didn't like what he had to do. It made him feel lower than a slug. He hoped his plan would work, and he prayed Sapphire never discovered how he'd been set up.

Chapter 2

Parker James slid his ID card into the lock of the steel door of the embassy basement room. When the mechanism popped open, he pushed open the heavy door and strolled into the secured room. He tried to appear casual as he walked over to the desks where Greg Williams and Anthony Neil were working.

"How's it going?" Parker directed his question to Anthony, the more approachable of the two men. "Find any new leads?" He wanted to know how far the team had progressed in their investigation of the ROSES leak.

Tony Neil glanced up, a welcoming smile on his youthful face. "Maybe."

Parker turned to the other man. Greg Williams had none of the gung-ho, youthful excitement that Tony, his partner, possessed. The weariness in Greg's eyes told Parker this man had been through a lot. But it was his pantherlike attitude—patient and deadly, as if waiting for his victim to get close enough—that unnerved people in the embassy.

There was something about Greg Williams that seemed familiar to Parker. He couldn't put his finger on it, but it nagged at him like a sore tooth. But that couldn't be, he told himself, since Greg had only been assigned to the embassy six months ago with the new rotation of staff. Parker had even gone so far as to check out Greg's personnel file. All the information matched what he'd been told by his superiors at the CIA.

"I stopped by to see if you two would like to go to lunch." Hopefully he could pry a little more information out of Tony and Greg while they ate.

"Yeah," Tony answered, putting down the folder he held. "I'm starved. What do you have in mind?"

"There's a Mexican restaurant around the block from here. It's a favorite of the embassy personnel. I thought we might go there." He rested his hip on the corner of Greg's desk and glanced at the computer screen. "You haven't been to Santa Fe Station, have you, Greg?"

The man's expression was guarded. "Can't say that I have." Immediately he saved what he was looking at and turned off his machine.

Parker stood. "Well, you're in for a treat. Mexican food prepared the way it would be if you were in Texas. I think you'll like it."

Greg Williams gave Parker a look that made him want to squirm.

"You think so?"

"Yeah."

Greg nodded. "Let's go."

* * *

Lauren checked the ice, making sure she had enough to get through the lunchtime rush. She prided herself in serving ice in her water and tea, a kind of welcome-home to the Americans living abroad. Satisfied there was enough, she picked up the menus and walked to the front of the restaurant.

"Parker, how nice to see you," she said, recognizing Jon's old associate. Parker had been a steadying force in her rocky world after her husband's death. He had often checked on her, taken her out to eat, listened to her woes.

"Lauren, I want you to meet two of my fellow workers." Parker stepped aside, and for the first time Lauren saw the two men standing behind him. Her field of vision narrowed to the face of the man who had appeared in her apartment and claimed to be her husband. When she'd awakened this morning, she had wondered if she had dreamt the entire episode. But here he was *in the flesh.*

"This—" Parker pulled the younger man forward "—is Tony Neil. And the guy beside him is Greg Williams."

"It's a pleasure to make your acquaintance," Tony said, shaking her hand.

The other man simply nodded.

With not so much as a blink of an eye did the man calling himself Greg Williams acknowledge he had met her. His warning of last night to tell no one of their meeting came to mind. So what was he doing here? Was this a test to see if she could keep her mouth shut?

More of this spy stuff, she thought sourly. Well, she could play that little game.

"This way, gentlemen."

After seating them, she turned to Greg. "Is this your first visit to Santa Fe Station?"

His brown eyes—not blue—returned the stare. "Yes, it is," he calmly answered.

Liar. If he was Jon, as he claimed, he had once been such a fixture at the restaurant that one of the waiters had joked that she should pay him for all the odd jobs he'd done around the place. And if he wasn't, then he'd lied to her last night, which fired her anger all over again. After the man left her apartment, Lauren had lain awake most of the night wondering why this man would claim to be her husband. She didn't have an answer but she couldn't believe he was telling the truth.

"Can you believe that Greg's been at the embassy for six months and hasn't found this place before now?" Parker asked.

As close as her restaurant was to the Grosvenor Street location, it was darn hard for Lauren to believe Greg hadn't stumbled across her place unless he had purposely avoided it. "Yes, I find that amazing."

A muscle in Greg's jaw jumped, but his irritation didn't deter her. She'd give him something to clamp his jaw around. "Let me recommend the chicken enchiladas with green sauce."

"I don't know if Greg wants to plunge in that deep his first time here," Parker interjected. "That's one of the hottest items on the menu."

"Is that so?" Greg asked.

She wanted to clobber him. "Yes. But then, if you're going to live life to the fullest, you have to take a few chances."

The impostor didn't flinch. "Well, for the time being, I'll take my chances in other areas. For now, I'll take the chili *rellenos* with salsa on the side."

This man was good, whoever he was. Although Jon had loved chicken enchiladas with green sauce, his passion for chili *rellenos* smothered in salsa was a close second.

"I'll send a waiter over to take your order." She smiled at Tony. "I hope you enjoy your meal."

"What about me?" Greg asked.

"I'll make sure the cook gives special attention to your food."

"I just bet you will," he mumbled.

He heard the key in the front-door lock. Closing her diary, which had proved to be interesting reading, he slipped it back into place under her lingerie and turned off the light on the nightstand.

The outer door closed, then immediately two thuds sounded against the floor, followed by a moan of relief. He smiled. The lady had just kicked off her shoes.

He plastered himself against the wall, waiting for her to come into the bedroom. If Lauren was consistent, she'd go into the living room, throw her mail on the chair, retrieve a soda from the icebox and take down her waist-length hair from the bun at the back of her head as she walked to the bedroom to change.

He was going to impress on her the need for safety, and her performance this afternoon was exactly the opposite of what she needed to do. Her actions had left Parker giving him odd looks the balance of the day.

The prank she had pulled on him at lunch might have blown up in his face. Lauren had kept her promise and had somehow tampered with the chili *relleno*. It tasted as though she'd loaded it with extra chili powder and spices. He'd fought the tears that formed in his eyes, not wanting Parker to know something was wrong. If he had caught on to the fact Lauren had purposely loaded the *relleno* with chili powder, Parker might wonder why she had it in for Greg Williams, whom she supposedly had never seen before in her life.

The light from the living room flicked on, then he heard her steps in the kitchen. The refrigerator door opened and closed. Her footsteps came closer. His muscles tensed as her shadow appeared in the doorway. The instant she walked into the room, he stepped forward on his good leg. One of his arms snaked around her waist, the other around her neck.

She shrieked, dropping her can of soda. Instantly his hand covered her mouth. She didn't meekly surrender, but instead drove her elbow into his belly and rammed her heel into the arch of his foot. He staggered back, knocking his cane, which had been resting against the bureau, into the hall.

The only thing that saved him from total collapse was that she'd already kicked off her shoes, so the blow to his foot was minimal. Damn, he should've remembered she'd taken several self-defense courses.

"Lauren, it's me, Jon," he whispered frantically into her ear. He hoped to reassure and calm her. Unfortunately his words seemed to have the opposite effect. She renewed her struggle.

He tightened his grip on her waist, hauling her flush against his body. "Lauren, stop it. I won't hurt you."

She bit the hand covering her mouth and kicked him in his bad knee. The blow caused his leg to buckle, and he was unable to keep them from crashing to the floor. He tried to cushion the fall for her by shifting his body under hers. He took the brunt of the impact on his shoulder, but he heard her cry of pain when she bounced off his body, then hit the wooden floor.

When his breath returned and he could speak again, he cursed, "Dammit, Lauren, why did you do that?"

She rolled over and faced him. Pushing her hair out of her face, she glared at him. "Me? Me?" She sat up. "You've got the gall to ask me why I fought some unseen attacker who grabbed me?"

"I told you who I was."

She rolled her eyes. "And that was supposed to reassure me?"

"Yes. I would never hurt you."

"You have a funny way of showing it."

He noticed then that she had unbuttoned her blouse before coming into the bedroom, and it hung open, giving him an unobstructed view of the peach lace that covered her beautiful breasts.

Noting the direction of his gaze, she glanced down and quickly pulled together the edges of her blouse. "What are you doing here? And how did you get in? I know I locked the French doors."

"Indeed you did. Only that lock isn't worth the cheap metal it's made of. You need to have it replaced."

"You're right. I need to replace it to keep out riffraff. Now, why are you here?"

"I came here to talk about our little meeting this afternoon." He struggled to sit up. Pain shot through his shoulder and down his side. A moan rose from his throat.

She came to her knees and reached out, touching his arm. "Are you okay?" Her green eyes darkened with concern.

He gave her a self-deprecating smile. "I'm getting too old for this kind of stuff."

She snorted. "Oh, please. If an eighteen-year-old had taken that fall, he would've been in pain." Standing, she held out her hand. "Come on."

He wondered if she planned any more karate moves.

"I'm not going to take you down a second time. You need to be out of here before my fiancé arrives."

A streak of jealousy shot through him. "Why's he showing up here?" He sounded like a covetous teenager.

She moved to the nightstand and turned on the light. "Not that it's any of your business, but he's taking me to our engagement party. His father is giving it."

"You're still planning on committing bigamy after what I told you last night?"

She placed her hands on her hips. The action made her blouse fly open again. Her hands gathered up the edges. "It will be bigamy only if your story is true."

"And you don't believe me?"

She opened her mouth, then closed it. "I have my doubts."

"How can I erase those doubts?"

Her gaze locked with his, and he read her desire to believe him, then the confusion that quickly followed. "Why are you here?"

The urge to touch her, to kiss that slim column of her neck, overwhelmed him. He took a step toward her, but his left knee gave out and he stumbled forward into her arms. She steadied him, then helped him sit on the bed.

"Where's your cane?" she asked, looking around.

"Look in the hall. I think in our wrestling match you knocked it out there."

"Which is exactly what you deserved," she said, bending to retrieve the oddly shaped cane. "Now, will you answer—"

The door chime rang, cutting off her question.

Frowning, she muttered, "That can't be Donald. It's too early. And he's never early."

She started down the hall with the cane in one hand, her other hand buttoning her blouse. He heard the door open.

"Parker, what are you doing here?"

Jon's blood ran cold.

"I came by to see you. You seemed upset this afternoon. I thought I'd check on you."

There was an awkward silence. Jon struggled to his feet and moved as quietly as he could to the door.

"Uh..." Lauren stumbled. "I'm not dressed for company or I would invite you in."

"I understand. I just wanted to make sure you were okay."

Jon prayed that Lauren had the cane out of sight. He didn't need for anyone at the embassy to know he was here.

"I appreciate your concern, Parker." Her voice softened when she said his name. "Donald is coming by to take me to our engagement party, and I need to hurry and change."

"I'm glad you're remarrying. You deserve to be happy after all your pain."

Guilt gripped Jon's heart.

"Thanks," she answered.

"Now, you're sure nothing happened to upset you?" Jon heard Parker ask. The man was being too persistent. Did he suspect something?

"I'm sure. I enjoyed meeting your friends today. But I will confess, the guy with the cane sent a chill up my spine. He has a sinister look."

Lauren was going to blow everything to hell. That's why he was here, to tell her not to indicate in any manner that they had had contact.

Parker laughed. "Yeah, Greg has that effect on people. They give him a wide berth."

Jon started to peek around the door.

"Lauren, did you spill your drink?"

Jon flattened himself back against the wall.

There was a pause, and he pictured Lauren glancing over her shoulder. "I was trying to change my outfit and drink at the same time. I dropped the can, and it rolled into the hall. I haven't had time to clean it up yet. I do need to hurry, Parker. Thanks for coming by."

The door closed and Jon slumped in relief. A moment later she appeared in the doorway.

"Here's your cane." She shoved it in his face.

"Did Parker see it?"

She arched her brow. "I may not be a spy, but I'm not stupid."

The corner of his mouth kicked up. "I take it that means that Parker didn't see it."

"You're good." The moment the words were out of her mouth, she flushed.

Devilry danced in his eyes. "You always thought so."

"Stop it. Why are you here?"

He took a step toward her, his cane supporting his weight. "To warn you again not to tell anyone about me or even to indicate you've met me. You almost gave it away at lunch, and then again a few moments ago. I think Parker might be suspicious."

Her eyes went cold. "And why should I listen to anything you say? You could be and probably are lying through your teeth."

Cupping her chin, he whispered, "Because, sweetheart, your life could depend on it." His lips settled on hers. They were soft, welcoming, and he felt alive for the first time in years. But he wanted more. "Open your mouth for me."

Her eyes flew open, and she jerked away from him. "Get out." She hugged herself.

"Lauren—"

"Now."

Her posture was defensive, and he knew she was in no mood to listen to further arguments.

"All right, I'm leaving. But remember my warning. Don't let anyone know I've contacted you."

Her eyes turned the color of storm-tossed seas. "Don't worry. I'll go on as if you never appeared."

And that was what he was afraid of.

Lauren gritted her teeth and nodded politely to the elderly couple who had just offered their congratulations on her engagement. She glanced around the fashionable room at the Blake family residence, noting all the elegantly garbed people gaily chatting with each other. The rich room went with the rich people. Soon she'd be married and live in this very house—that is, unless Jon/Greg's claims were true. The thought of marrying Donald Blake disturbed her, and the appearance of Jon/Greg was only partially to blame.

"You look marvelous, my dear," Donald whispered in her ear. Donald and his father owned a catering company that contracted with several large firms in London and Brussels to run their cafeterias. She'd met Donald at a convention for restaurateurs a year and a half ago.

"That silver dress makes you look like you're wrapped in a cloud," he continued, placing his damp hand on her bare shoulder.

And her expression probably made her look like a thunderhead, she thought as she glanced down at the yards and yards of chiffon.

"Are you having a good time?"

No, she wanted to shout. I just want to go home and stew about the man who popped into my flat the last two nights, claiming to be my husband. Instead, she said, "It's a lovely party. Your firm always serves the best buffet I've ever tasted."

Donald beamed. He was a nice-looking man, pale, with red hair and soft blue eyes, and a complete opposite from Jonathan. She often wondered if the reason she'd been attracted to Donald was that he was so different from Jon in every way. Suddenly the safe refuge of Donald's unflappable temperament wasn't as appealing as it had been two nights ago.

"Oh, darling, there's someone I need to talk to. I'll be back in a minute." He didn't wait for a response. He simply kissed her cheek and waded through the crowd.

With a sigh of resignation, Lauren watched him walk away. Donald was a good, steady man, but business was his passion.

A uniformed waiter passed, and she set her empty glass on the tray. "Do you have any more ginger ale?"

The waiter nodded to the glass set apart from the others. "I brought you a refill."

Lauren smiled at the man. All of Donald's staff were aware she was allergic to alcohol. She blushed, remembering the party given for a French industrialist where she'd had a glass of champagne at Donald's urging. He hadn't believed her when she told him she was allergic to alcohol. His reasoning had been she hadn't had true French champagne, and no one would have a bad reaction to such magnificent stuff. Ten minutes later she'd been as sick as a dog and disgraced herself in front of the Frenchman. Since then, Donald and all his employees only offered her nonalcoholic drinks.

With her glass clutched in one hand, Lauren sought a quiet place where she could be alone for a few minutes. She strode down the dimly lit hall until she came to the library. A single light glowed from a lamp on the desk.

"Hello," she called. No one answered. The room was empty. Relieved to be alone at last, she settled into the leather chair behind the massive desk and sipped her drink. After a few minutes of peace, she stood, ready to rejoin the party. As she moved around the corner of the desk, her hip caught a book and knocked it to the floor. Bending to retrieve it, she noticed a piece of blue paper sticking out. She pulled it from the book and read. At first she thought it was scrap, since the doodling on the paper made no sense, so she turned over the sheet. The names of several corporations were listed. And beside each name was a different single word: "red," "code," "base," "trigger."

How odd, she thought, replacing the paper inside the book. After straightening the pile of books on the desk corner, she picked up her drink and rejoined the party.

From a chair deep in the shadows of the room, a match flared to life. A man narrowed his eyes as he lighted the end of his cigar. Lauren had seen his shopping list. He knew it had been careless of him to leave it in that book, but who would've thought anyone would find it even accidentally?

Had she understood what she'd seen? the man wondered. He had never been comfortable with Parker's assumption that Lauren didn't know anything about her husband's CIA activities. She might have some contact within the agency to whom she would pass the information she'd just seen.

The man hesitated in his decision. He didn't want to eliminate her, but she would have to be watched even more carefully than she had been over the past three years.

Perhaps, he thought, he'd arrange for her to have a few minor accidents to see what happened. To see if anyone came to her rescue. And if someone from the agency did, he vowed silently it would be that person's last act on earth.

Jon knocked on the door of Tony's flat. He was excited by Tony's call claiming that he'd cracked the ROSES ring. If Tony had, he knew it might lead to identifying the mole within the London station. He knocked again. Nothing.

"Tony?" he called out. No response.

Cautiously he wrapped his fingers around the doorknob and turned. It opened easily. He didn't rush in but peered through the crack between the door and frame. When he was satisfied no one was hiding behind it, he entered the flat.

Several steps into the room, Jon spotted Tony's body sprawled facedown on the floor, a pool of blood under his friend's chest. He knelt on his good knee and pressed his fingers against the carotid artery in Tony's neck. Nothing, not a hint of life.

He glanced around the room. The computer was on, but the screen displayed only an error message, "Unable to open drive a." There was no disk in the machine. Items from the desk were scattered on the floor and around Tony's body.

Jon started to rise, but saw a shadow on the floor. Before he could move, something heavy connected with the back of his head. As the floor rushed up to meet him and darkness closed in, Jon thought he saw a pair of cowboy boots.

Jon's head throbbed as his mind struggled up from the deep fog. In the distance he thought he heard a woman screaming.

"Oh, Bob, there's a dead man. Call the police." He heard footsteps retreating.

Jon turned his head to the side and saw Tony's dead body. He struggled to sit up. It was then he noticed the gun in his hand. He cursed.

Sirens wailed in the distance. Jon knew he needed to get out before the police showed up. He got to his feet and glanced around the room, searching for something that would give him a clue to the killer's true identity.

Nothing. Not one damn clue, except that the killer wore cowboy boots.

The sirens were coming closer. Jon slid the gun into his shirt to dispose of later. With a final silent goodbye to his friend, he slipped out of the apartment... and bumped into a woman in the hall.

"Oh, oh—" She screamed and rushed into her flat. "It's the killer, Bob," she cried.

Thankfully no one tried to stop Jon as he left the building and headed toward the embassy. He hoped to get to the files before whoever had killed Tony did.

Chapter 3

"Stupid man," Lauren grumbled as she searched through the mound of papers on her desk for the gas bill. Her office desk, tucked into the corner of the small room at the rear of her restaurant, was no neater than her desk at home.

"Who does he think he is, barging into my life, turning everything inside out, then disappearing?"

She found the bill and slapped it down by her open checkbook.

It had been three days since the man calling himself Jonathan Michaels mysteriously appeared in her apartment a second time, then, just as mysteriously, disappeared. Three days of jumping every time a person walked into the restaurant, every time the phone rang. Her cook, Jimmy Mason—a crusty young man from Liverpool—was ready to strangle her. He'd threatened to take every ounce of chili powder in the place and dump it in the Thames if she walked into his kitchen just one more time this afternoon. She didn't doubt he would.

Lauren flipped a strand of her dark brown hair over her shoulder. She'd been late to work this morning and had not bothered to pin up her waist-length hair in its usual bun. Her mother thought that at the age of twenty-nine, Lauren was too old to have such long hair. But it was Lauren's one vanity, and she refused to cut it.

Her mood wasn't improved any by remembering the stupid accident she'd had yesterday. She had raced into the alley to catch the meat-delivery man when a stack of heavy wooden crates had fallen. She'd moved fast enough to prevent any real injury, but one of the crates had caught her just above her left wrist, leaving an ugly bruise.

Lauren picked up her pen and wrote a check for the amount of the gas bill. After sealing the envelope, she added it to the pile of letters to mail.

"Lauren." The yell came from the hall. "Open the door or I'll toss this package."

She hurried across the room and pulled open the door. Jimmy's head bobbed above the box.

"My package from Santa Fe," she cried with delight. Jimmy placed the box on the corner of her desk. "Right ye are."

Grabbing the letter opener off the blotter, she nudged Jimmy out of the way with her hip. Jimmy and Lauren were the same height, five foot six, but he outweighed her by forty pounds.

"Look, Jimmy." Lauren motioned to him. "Look at all these wonderful spices." She eagerly dug through the box until she came to a clear bag filled with a lavender blue powder. "Here it is." She held the sack high. "Blue cornmeal."

"Ugh. Nasty stuff—that business."

"Yours is an untrained palate."

He snorted. "I'm the cook."

"A minor point." She stuffed the blue cornmeal into her purse, then picked up the letters. "I'm going to post these. I'll be back in twenty minutes."

The sun shone, unusual for October, through the watery clouds. Lauren loved London. Unlike most Americans, she enjoyed walking and taking the bus, freeing her from having to put up with her cranky '72 MG convertible.

After posting her letters, she stopped by the newsstand several feet from the entrance to her restaurant. As she reached for the *London Times,* her eyes fastened on the day's headline, and she froze.

American Official Killed.

She scanned the other papers on the kiosk, and each carried the same story. Grabbing the *Times,* she paid, then began to read the story.

Anthony Neil, an American embassy officer, was found dead in his London apartment early this morning from a gunshot wound. Authorities are searching for Greg Williams, a fellow embassy worker, for questioning. He was seen leaving Mr. Neil's residence early Wednesday morning.

Lauren didn't read any further. Instead, her eyes slid to the picture of the suspect beside the article. It was a picture of the man who called himself Jon Michaels.

Oblivious to the people around her, she leaned against a streetlight. The smell of petrol and the roar of passing engines penetrated her shock. She glanced up in time to see a red Ford Escort racing toward her. Her numb mind refused to work, and for a split second she watched in grim fascination as the car seemed to advance in slow motion.

A strong hand seized her upper arm and pulled her back just as the front wheel of the Ford jumped the curb and clipped the corner of the kiosk, causing it to tip sideways, then collapse. The car sped off, leaving the kiosk owner yelling profanities and Lauren gasping at the near miss she had just had.

She turned, ready to thank her rescuer, but the words died in her throat. Above her towered Jon. Or Greg. Or whatever he was calling himself today. He clumsily pulled her across the sidewalk into the alley, then jerked her into the building next to the restaurant. When she tried to free her arm, he fiercely whispered, "Stop it. I'll explain everything later."

His large scarred hand slid down her arm to manacle her wrist, but his hold, surprisingly, did not hurt. For some obscure reason, she was not afraid. Annoyed. Angry. But not afraid. Perhaps it was his limp, or the cane he leaned on, that dissipated her fear.

He led her down several hallways, then pushed her into the small space of an inset door. He glanced over both shoulders, his eyes sweeping the empty corridor, before turning back to her.

"What's the matter with you, staring at that car racing toward you and not trying to get out of its way?"

"What's the matter with me?" she choked angrily. "You—that's what's wrong with me. Seeing your picture in the paper as an accused killer rather set me off my stride." She shook the damning article in his face.

He plucked the paper from her hands, hooked the cane over his forearm and read the story. He uttered a pithy curse that made Lauren's ears burn. His eyes met hers. "I didn't kill him. I was set up."

At the sound of footsteps, he fell silent but the worry on his face told her they were still in danger. He reached for the door behind Lauren, but the knob resisted. Without a word he gathered her in his arms and his lips covered hers.

It was like lightning had struck. Every nerve ending in Lauren's body tingled, and her stomach seemed to be doing somersaults. Her hands came up and clutched his shoulders to steady herself. She barely heard the snickers of the passing people. Instead, all her senses were focused on the warm mouth devouring hers. When he drew back, a whimper escaped her lips. His hand ran down the silky length of her hair.

"I love your hair," he breathed into her ear.

A discreet cough broke into their little world. "Excuse me." A tall, thin man stood near them craning his neck, as if his collar was suddenly two sizes too small. "I need to open my office."

Lauren buried her head into Jon's chest, unable to face the stranger. "I'll get you for this," she mumbled into his blue shirt.

She felt—actually felt—Jon's satisfied grin. "Of course. You must excuse our behavior. We were just married about an hour ago."

A sick feeling replaced her earlier euphoria. The easy manner in which this man dissembled was disturbing. If he lied so easily and convincingly to this stranger, couldn't he have just as easily lied to her?

The tight expression on the man's face relaxed, and he winked at Jon. "I understand. I hope you feel the same in ten years."

Jon pulled Lauren away from the door into the hall. "I'm sure I will." He wrapped his arm around her waist and guided her away from the witness.

Lauren stiffened her body, trying to dig in her heels. With the highly polished black-and-white tile floor and muscles in his arms the size of Arnold Schwarzenegger's, her resistance had no effect, in spite of his awkward gait.

"Where are you taking me?" she challenged.

"If you want us both to live out the day, you'll cooperate," Jon replied.

"If you want to live long enough to leave this building, you'll take your hands off me and explain," she swore between clenched teeth.

"Lauren, we don't have time to play twenty questions. Whoever was in that red Ford didn't intend to miss. They'll be back."

"Back for who?"

His eyes darkened with pain. "I don't know. The guy in the Ford could've seen me walking up to where you stood. He could've been after me."

From his tone, she knew there was more. "Go on. What else do you suspect?"

"I can't discard any possibility, no matter how much I dislike it."

Lauren wanted to shout her frustrations. This man was not a fount of information. "What possibility occurs to you?"

He grasped her hand and lightly ran his fingers over her wrist. She winced. Glancing down, he frowned at the sight of the bruise above her wrist. "What happened?"

She shrugged. "Just a freak accident at the restaurant."

His head jerked up, and he pinned her with a hard, no-nonsense stare. "What kind of accident?"

"Some crates in the alley toppled over."

"Are you sure it was an accident?"

"Of course." But suddenly Lauren wasn't so sure. With all the crazy things that had happened in the past few days, anything was possible. "You never answered my question, but then you're good at doing that."

He lightly squeezed her hand. "Who else was standing there on the street, sweetheart?"

"Me?" Her voiced echoed down the hall.

He didn't verbally respond, but the answer was there in his gaze.

"Why on earth would anyone want to kill me?"

He released her. "Remember I warned you that the mole might go after you to flush me out into the open. That's why I kept warning you to be cautious."

Chills raced down her spine.

"Lauren, I need to contact my superior in Washington and tell him what's happened. But I need to find someplace safe and private to call from. Someplace where I can be reached later on today." He ran his fingers through his hair, ruffling the thick strands.

"How about my apartment?" The words popped out of her mouth, surprising her, and him, judging from his expression. This man's story was beyond belief, yet on some deep, instinctive level she trusted him. It would be the height of folly for her to trust this man, she admonished herself. His story had so many holes in it, it resembled Swiss cheese. But if this man was really Jon and she turned her back on him and he was hurt or killed, she wouldn't be able to live with herself.

Of course, the fact that he set her heart racing and turned her knees to mush had nothing to do with her decision, she firmly told herself.

"No," he said, startling her out of her thoughts. "Someone might have seen me at your apartment. I was afraid that I might have blown my cover contacting you. That little incident out on the street makes me think I did."

She didn't buy his argument, but from his expression he believed it. "What about a hotel?"

"With my picture plastered all over the front page of every London paper?"

"Your place?"

His brow raised in a disapproving gesture.

"Listen, I'm not real adept at this spy stuff," she grumbled. Mentally she ran through the list of her friends. "Jimmy. We can use his place."

"Jimmy?"

She didn't like the dubious look in his eyes or the dark tone of his voice. "My cook. And you can take that indignant note out of your voice. He's a good friend and nothing more, not that it's any concern of yours."

Jon stepped closer and grasped her arm. "But it is my concern. Suddenly I've discovered I'm a very possessive husband."

Something about his tone, the low, throbbing quality, stirred her blood. "Oh, sure, that's why you've been gone for three years," she blurted, irritated that she felt so strong a reaction.

His hand covered hers, his thumb stroking her wrist. "I've already explained about that. I couldn't have returned sooner. It would've put you in unnecessary danger." He shook his head. "Except on that score it seems I failed anyway."

She turned away from his penetrating stare and looked around for a public phone. When she located one on the wall by the outside door, she strode toward it. She dialed the number of her restaurant. Jimmy quickly agreed to Lauren's plan.

After hanging up, she turned to Jon. "Everything's settled. Jimmy's flat is in Hammersmith. There's an Underground station close by that we can use," she said. "But I want some explanations once we're there. No hedging, no lies, no half truths. Deal?"

He studied her for a long moment. At first she thought he'd refuse, but he shrugged and nodded.

As they walked to the station, in the opposite direction from her restaurant, she thought she heard him mumble, "If it's truth she wants, truth she'll get, warts and all."

Lauren acutely felt Jon's tension as they walked toward the Marble Arch Station to catch the Underground. He held her right hand in his left, making sure he was always the one closest to the street. Even if he hadn't had a cane, she knew he would put her on his left side. She had a cousin in the military who had told her that it was customary for the man to take this position in order to protect his escort.

Jon's eyes constantly moved over the street, and he was alert to all that was going on around them. How alert was brought home to her when he steered her around a wad of chewing gum on the sidewalk.

"Can't have you leaving tracks," he murmured, leaning close.

She stared at him with wide eyes. Who was this guy? Superman, with X-ray vision? She hoped not. Her underwear was in no condition to be viewed.

Once aboard the correct train, Lauren breathed a sigh of relief. Before she could settle back in her seat, Jon's arm slipped around her waist, anchoring her to his side, and he began to nibble her ear. She tried to jerk away, but his arm tightened around her in warning.

"What do you think you're doing?" she whispered furiously.

He didn't raise his face from her neck. "Look at the man across the aisle."

She glanced at the figure hidden by the paper. "What the...?" Her voice trailed off as she realized Jon's picture stared back at her from the front page of the newspaper the man held. "Oh, my."

He snorted. "My sentiments exactly."

"Why can't he fold his paper inside out like any other good Englishman?" she asked, her mouth puckering with annoyance.

"Now do you understand my need to keep my face hidden?" He raised his head slightly.

Her eyes slid to Jon's face. The corners of his mouth were tight and his eyes harsh with strain.

"Yes," she whispered.

Her answer relaxed him, and he rested his head on her shoulder, making sure his face was concealed by her long hair.

Lauren tried to ignore his warm breath fanning the skin behind her ear. She looked out the window, but the inky blackness speeding by did not distract her.

Who was this man? And what was she doing here with him? For all she knew, he could be an escaped mental patient. That wasn't beyond the realm of possibility.

No, he wasn't crazy. He was running.

The man across from them had finally folded his paper and was working on the crossword puzzle. Before she could tell Jon, firm lips touched her neck. She nearly jumped out of her seat.

"He's put up the paper," she said softly as her fingers curled into her palm.

"I know."

"You're enjoying this too much."

"You're right."

She turned and glared. "Don't push your luck."

He gave her a brief squeeze. "I'm sorry to put you through this, Lauren."

"Then control your hormones."

His eyes narrowed as he studied her. Lauren tried not to squirm but lost the battle when she adjusted her shoulders and looked away.

"I'm not the only one with raging hormones, am I?" Amusement colored his words.

The muscles of her jaw tightened, and she raised her chin.

The lights from the upcoming station pierced their tense silence.

Jon glanced at the lighted sign in the tunnel. "Is this the right station?"

Lauren gathered her purse and stood. "Yes."

He clamped his hand around her wrist. Lauren glanced down in surprise.

"Stay close. If anyone recognizes me, I want you to run as fast as those gorgeous legs will carry you. Don't go back to your apartment. If for some reason we get separated, I'll contact you through your restaurant."

His words sent a chill through her. They were not playing at being spies. This was real, with the stakes life and death.

As they walked up the stairs to street level, Lauren anxiously studied each individual who passed close to them.

"I wish I had some sort of weapon," she said as they emerged onto the street.

"You do. That tongue of yours can neatly slice an opponent to ribbons."

She considered the possibility of kicking him in the shins, then disregarded it. His legs had already suffered too much injury for her to add to it. "I meant a more conventional weapon, such as a gun."

"You're safe with me."

"Says who?"

"I'll explain once we're at your cook's apartment."

They turned down a quiet side street. At the fourth set of concrete steps, she turned in. Jimmy's flat was on the second floor in the rear of the building. Although Jon tried not to show it, Lauren saw him favor his right leg as he climbed the stairs.

"How do you plan on getting in?" Jon asked as they walked down the carpeted hall.

"His neighbor keeps a key."

Within minutes they were inside. Any doubts Lauren had about Jon's profession were demolished by his careful inspection of the place. He surveyed each room, walking through it, checking the locks on the windows and the view each one afforded. After prowling about for five minutes, he joined Lauren in the living room.

"I don't want to be taken by surprise. First rule of spying is always know the lay of the place and the potential escape routes."

"Oh, I thought it was 'never tell the truth, especially to your spouse.'"

"So you're admitting I am Jon."

"Let's just say I'm putting my doubts on hold." She adjusted her skirt around her legs, trying to sort through her conflicting feelings. Her mind told her that this whole situation was contrived and untrue, yet her heart refused the logic. This man stirred her senses just as Jon had done. The chemistry between them couldn't be denied. Yet when she thought about it, she realized the only D she'd received in college had been in Chemistry, so maybe she was deceiving herself. Besides, whatever happened to her rule about not dating liars? She'd learned from her mother's painful experiences with three husbands that lies were always hurtful, and if Lauren caught a man lying to her, she never dated him again.

She threw Jon a questioning look as he settled on the opposite end of the plaid couch, his cane between his legs. For the first time she studied it. Rubber tipped, the highly polished black wood did not curve to form a natural handle. Instead, the wood ended abruptly, and the golden handle was at a ninety-degree angle from the shaft.

He reached for the phone on the side table and dialed. From the number of digits, it seemed to be a local call, but he waited an extraordinary length of time to speak.

"Diamond, this is Sapphire. Tony's been killed, and I've been set up as the prime suspect. We need to talk. I'll call again at 2200 hours my time."

Replacing the handset into the cradle, he glanced at her.

"More spy lingo?"

He shrugged.

"Why didn't you tell him where you were, or at least give him the number here?"

"You never know who might listen to the answering-machine tape."

The seriousness of the situation in which she found herself stared Lauren in the face. "I need some plausible answers, Jon or Greg or whoever."

He had the gall to grin. "Why don't you call me Jon?"

"Another name comes to mind," she answered.

He wagged his finger at her. "Tut, tut, Lauren. Your mother would be disappointed that her daughter would even consider using such language."

She wanted to shout at him to stop doing that. To stop reaching inside her soul and touching places that were still tender. Steeling herself against his seductive pull, she asked, "Why were you accused of killing Anthony Neil?"

"Because a woman wandered into Tony's flat and saw me sprawled on the floor with a gun in my hand. Tony's body was next to me."

"I'd say she had reason."

"I didn't do it. Late last night Anthony called, said he'd figured out how the spy ring—code-named ROSES—worked. We are trying to connect a series of burglaries in defense contractors working with NATO. I told him I'd be right over." He shook his head and explained what happened at Tony's flat.

He stood and walked to the window. After checking the street, he returned to the couch, sitting close to Lauren. He didn't lean back but sat on the edge of the cushions, his hands hanging loosely between his thighs. His cane rested against his shoulder.

His fingers slid up and down the smooth surface of his cane as his gaze focused on the opposite wall. Touched by the pain in his eyes, she laid her hand on his arm. Startled, he looked down.

"What did you do after you left your partner's place? And what happened to the gun?" Her unspoken acceptance of his story brought light to his troubled eyes.

"I went back to the embassy to get our copies of the files we were working on. But the police and embassy security were out in number, and I couldn't get inside." He sighed. "By now I'm sure the mole has read through the information we had on the spy ring."

"Didn't you or Anthony have backup disks?"

"I made a copy of the control disk and hid it in my apartment. When I tried to retrieve it, the police were there, questioning my neighbors. I was able to see inside my apartment through the living room windows. It had been searched, and I don't think it was the police who trashed the place. The probability of my backup disk still being there is low."

Lauren felt completely helpless. What could she do to prove or disprove his story? And if he was telling the truth, how could she help him? She'd failed to take Spying 101 at the University of Texas and didn't know the first thing about spooks.

"You still trying to figure out if I'm telling the truth?"

"Yes. You didn't tell me what you did with the gun."

"I wiped my prints off and threw it in the Thames. All I needed was to be stopped by some bobby and found with the murder weapon on my body. It looks bad now, but if that had happened, I would've been staring at the inside walls of the local jail."

His story was outrageous, and she had to be crazy to believe him.

Suddenly, as if he could read her thoughts, he leaned close and his mouth brushed hers, sending sparks of pleasure rushing over her skin.

"Trust your heart, Lauren. It's never failed you before."

His comment hit a nerve. She jumped off the couch and faced him. "You're wrong. The biggest mistake of my life was trusting my heart and marrying you."

Chapter 4

The man claiming to be Jonathan Michaels sighed as he watched Lauren move to the window. She wrapped her arms around her waist, staring out into the street. Her body language told him clearly that she was hurting inside. And he knew he was the cause of that hurt. He never wanted to cause her a moment of anguish, but it seemed that all he did was wound her.

"Damn," he swore savagely.

Lauren jumped at the expletive. Her eyes locked with his, and Jon wanted to erase the pain he saw in her beautiful green eyes. What could he say to make things right? What could he do?

The ugly realization that there was nothing he could do hit him like an iron fist on the chin.

The growling of Lauren's stomach broke the tense moment.

She shrugged. "I haven't eaten today," she explained. "I was late to work and skipped breakfast. I intended to eat after posting my letter, only things didn't go exactly as I planned.''

Jon felt the barb in her words. ''I know the feeling. Things haven't gone as I planned for a long time.'' He gave her a sad smile, hoping she would read his regret in involving her in this mess.

Her expression softened. ''Let's see what Jimmy has to eat.'' She strode to the kitchen and began a careful search of the cabinets. All she found was a box of cereal with a few crumbs at the bottom, a couple cans of soup, a can of sardines and a moldy loaf of bread.

''It appears that your cook takes most of his meals at the restaurant,'' Jon offered, surveying the green mass in the plastic package.

Lauren turned to Jon. ''You can have your sardines with or without mold.''

He nodded toward the refrigerator. ''What's in there?''

A single bottle of cream stood forlornly inside. ''Not much better.'' She started to close the door, then stopped. Quickly she pulled the cream from the interior, sniffed it to make sure it was okay. Satisfied it wasn't spoiled, she set it on the counter. ''We're going to have a feast.''

Jon frowned as she ran to her purse and retrieved a clear plastic bag. She held it up as if she had found a rare treasure. It was filled with a lavender blue powder. ''You're going to love this,'' she told him mischievously.

She filled a pot with water, tore open the package and threw in several handfuls of the blue powder.

''Dare I ask what it is you're fixing?'' he asked.

Lauren froze, her panic making any movement impossible. She had been so sure that this man was her husband. But the real Jonathan Michaels would have known what she was cooking. She had made it often while they were married. He had refused to eat the odd-colored cereal, teasing her unmercifully that the blob in her bowl looked like wallpaper paste and he did not want her lips glued together—he had better things to do with them.

"Mush." *Act casually,* she warned herself. *Don't give yourself away.*

"Blue mush?"

"You'll like it, wait and see."

She dished out the cereal into two bowls, stirred in sugar and poured the cream over the contents.

"Take a bite," she urged after setting the bowl on the table before him, trying to sound as if nothing was wrong.

Jon picked up his spoon. "Are you sure you're not trying to poison me?"

She nearly lost her fragile composure. "Here, I'll take the first taste." Quickly she scooped up a spoonful and placed it in her mouth. The familiar taste overwhelmed her fear. "Heavenly," she groaned. When she looked at Jon, his eyes were resting on her lips, and the hunger on his face had nothing to do with his stomach. His hunger awakened a corresponding sensation in her.

Disturbed by her mixed feelings of attraction and fear, Lauren sat up straighter. "Eat."

Slowly he brought the spoon, filled with mush, to his lips. His gaze never left her as his mouth closed around the smooth metal spoon. She looked away, unable to bear the sensual message in his eyes.

"How do you like it?" she asked after a moment.

"How do I like what?"

Her head snapped around, and her heart stopped at the fire dancing in his eyes.

"The blue-cornmeal mush."

"It's okay, but the taste of your lips would be better."

Lauren gulped. Her heart was pounding so hard in her chest, she wondered why he couldn't see the movement.

He took another bite, and his brow knitted. He reached behind him and grabbed the bag of meal. "You've fixed this for me before, haven't you?" He looked up expectantly.

"Yes."

He rubbed his temples. "After the accident I discovered there were holes in my memory. There were certain times, certain incidents, that I discovered I couldn't recall. As time has passed, most of the missing parts have been filled in."

Could she believe him? Memory loss was a convenient excuse, yet hadn't he sort of remembered she'd made the cereal before? Or had there been something in her manner to alert him? Her heart ached, and she wondered if she was the biggest fool walking the face of the earth; whatever the truth was, she had to acknowledge she was attracted to this handsome man, whoever—whatever—he was.

"Did you ever write *How Tall Is Red?*"

His question jerked her out of her thoughts. She considered denying she ever wanted to write a mystery, but it seemed like a moot point since the man already knew the title of the book. "No."

He set down his spoon and studied her. "That's a shame. I know that was a dream of yours. Holding on to dreams is important in this harsh world. If you can't dream, you lose hope.''

His comments were either a telling glimpse of his soul or a good diversion to keep her from asking if he knew the plot of her book and not simply the title. ''Why don't you tell me the plot?'' she said with a small smile.

''You're still doubting me, huh?''

If she believed him, his voice had been injured in the accident. The low, gravelly quality was as seductive as intimate words whispered in the dark of night. She cleared her throat. ''Let's just say I'm cautious.''

Folding his arms across his chest, he fixed her with an unsettling look. ''We were on the beach in Ayr. You were sitting between my legs, my arms were wrapped around your waist. We had just come from our little rented house where we had spent the afternoon making hot love.''

She jerked back in the chair. Vividly she remembered that afternoon, the glory and joy she'd shared with Jon. To be reminded of it now was like acid on her raw heart. ''I don't need a commentary on the day,'' she snapped. ''Just tell me the plot.''

He reached out for her hand, but she snatched it off the table, unable to deal with his touch when her heart was tearing in two. ''Are you going to tell me?'' she demanded, her hands tightly clasped in her lap.

It was clear from his expression that he wanted to continue pursuing the point of their intimacy, but he resigned himself to talking about the book. ''The reason I mention what happened is because that was the first time you admitted that you wanted to write mysteries. When I questioned you, all you had was the title of the book.'' He pushed away his half-eaten bowl of mush. ''The heroine's name was Rachel something....

She goes to an inn in Vermont for a vacation. A man stumbles into her room and mumbles, 'How tall is red?' Then he collapses and dies.''

Lauren tried to hold back the moan rising in her throat but was unsuccessful. This couldn't be happening. There had to be a logical explanation for him knowing about the book.

Leaning forward, he lightly brushed his fingers across her chin.

Sparks of electricity danced over her skin. She turned away from his touch. "Who was the hero?" she tightly asked.

His tired sigh filled the room, making Lauren aware that this man was trying to win her trust.

"His name was Sam MacKinnon, and he was the man to whom the dead man was trying to relay the information. 'How tall is red?' was the code phrase that Sam needed to hear so he could recognize his contact. Sam's response was to have been 'Tall enough to see over the wall.'"

Lauren didn't want to hear any more. He knew. He knew too much to be an impostor...and yet everything didn't fit together as it should. She stumbled away from the table, wanting to put as much distance as she could between her and this confusing man. She heard him stand, followed by a muffled noise. He cursed. Then it sounded like wood hitting metal. Lauren winced but refused to turn around and see if he was okay. She couldn't afford the softening of her heart if she saw him struggling with his cane. A moment later she felt his warm hands on her shoulders.

"Lauren."

She tried to shrug off his touch, but he wouldn't let go.

"Sweetheart." His lips brushed the back of her ear. "I don't know what else I can do to prove to you who I am, but it is important that you believe me."

"Quit lying to me. That would be a start."

"I haven't been, Lauren."

She glanced over her shoulder, not bothering to hide her skepticism. "Since when?"

He looked chagrined. "All right, you have a point. What I mean is that I haven't lied to you since I returned." He wrapped his arms around her waist and drew her back against his body. "Do you want me to tell you what I remember the most vividly about you?"

She stared straight ahead. "No."

He placed a kiss on the sensitive spot at the base of her neck above her collarbone. Shivers raced up and down her spine. Jon had found that spot on their wedding night and had used that knowledge to his advantage often and with relish. When he kissed her there, it never failed to make her knees weak, her heart race and her body want more.

"That's one of the things I remember about you, how that spot affected you. And there's a place beside your right hip that when I kissed it—"

Her heart couldn't take any more, and she began to fight against his restraining arms. "Let me go," she demanded.

His hold tightened. "No, I need you to believe me."

The cynical thought occurred to her that this man realized his error with the blue cornmeal and now was trying to smooth over his gaffe. Lauren considered driving her elbow into his stomach or kicking him in his bad knee, but somehow she couldn't bring herself to deliberately hurt him.

"Thank you, sweetheart."

She looked over her shoulder at him. He grinned down at her.

"Since I know you, it isn't hard to know what you were thinking. And I'm grateful you didn't kick me. I don't think my knee could've taken it."

"Then let me go."

"All right, but only if you promise me you'll kiss me."

"Why would I want to kiss you?"

"To prove to yourself who I am. You always told me that kissing me curled your toes. I figure the best way to prove my identity is lip to lip."

Lauren clearly remembered telling Jon that his kisses were like bottled lightning, making every nerve ending in her body tingle.

"Are you up to the challenge?" he asked. "Or do you still want to hold on to the idea I'm not Jonathan Michaels, your husband?"

"All right. I'll take your challenge."

His surprise showed clearly on his face. He nodded and released her. Turning to face him, she lifted her chin, waiting for him to kiss her.

A laugh rumbled in his chest. He leaned close and said, "Why don't you purse your lips and close your eyes like a virgin offering herself up as a sacrifice?"

Caught between laughter at the picture he portrayed and anger that he was mocking her doubts, Lauren said nothing. A gentle smile curved his mouth, and his hands cupped her face. Slowly he lowered his head to hers.

It was odd to kiss a man with a mustache and beard. His facial hair was soft and it tickled. But in spite of those distractions, Lauren felt something familiar, some old chemistry spring to life.

Wanting to move closer to the warmth of the man, Lauren slipped her arms around his waist. Jon raised his head and searched her eyes. His brown eyes burned brightly with passion, the same passion she felt. The color of his eyes threw her off. She was expecting to see Jon's blue eyes instead of brown ones.

"Do you know now?" He didn't wait for an answer but took her mouth again in a searing kiss. His tongue slipped inside, lightly caressing the inside of her lips, teeth and cheeks. Her confusion was zapped, like a wildfire bursting to life in the forest and consuming everything around it. Up to this point in her life, only Jon had been able to inspire this hot, out-of-control feeling. Was it possible that another man could spark this reaction in her?

He trailed kisses across her cheek and down her neck. "Ah, this is what I remember about you. Your sweet passion. When I was flat on my back in the hospital in France, I remembered how you responded to me. The little sounds you made and how they would always send me over the edge every time."

His words penetrated the red haze surrounding her brain like bright sunlight through fog. The guy was good. He knew all the strings to pull to get a reaction out of her. If he was an impostor, he deserved an Oscar. If he wasn't—

The shock of the realization, which had been building in her subconscious since he'd first reappeared, hit her hard. She jerked out of his embrace and backed away from him. Her feelings were racing around inside her like the winds of a tornado, with the same speed and intensity.

Her heart was saying, *Yes, he is Jon.* But her mind couldn't accept it.

Joy mixed with hurt. If he was Jon, then why had he let her think he was dead for the past three years? The question hammered her brain. Did he know the hell she'd gone through? Did he have any idea of the depression and grief she'd fought her way through and how hard it had been to put her life back together? And now he walked back into her life and everything was supposed to be peachy-keen, and they would go on as if nothing had happened?

The sense of betrayal nearly knocked her off her feet.

"Now do you believe me?" he asked.

"If I believed you to be Jonathan, I'd also have to hate you."

That brought a look of shock to his face.

"You want to know why?"

"I can guess," he replied sadly.

"It's taken me three years to put my life back together again. Three years of hell. And you stroll into my apartment, claim to be Jon, alive and well, and blow my neatly ordered life to pieces." Tears welled in her eyes, and she spun away from him, not wanting him to see her grief. "And do you know how much I hate liars? How my mother's husbands killed her by inches with their lies?"

"Lauren."

He laid his hand on her back, but she couldn't tolerate his touch without throwing herself in his arms and bawling like a baby.

"I wanted to let you know I was alive, but it would've been selfish of me."

She whirled. "Selfish? Would it have been selfish to spare me the pain?" She tapped her forehead with her fingers. "Forgive me, it's obvious."

"I deserve your cynicism."

"You're damn right you do."

He folded his arms across his chest and watched her. Lauren knew he was waiting for her to calm down enough to hear his explanation. She moved to the couch and sat.

"I'm ready to listen," she informed him. "But this had better be good."

He nodded. "The hardest thing I've done in my life was not contacting you. But I couldn't take the chance that the mole who betrayed me would hold you hostage if he discovered I was still alive." He sat next to her. "If you'd come to France, our killer would've followed you—of that I'm certain. I was in no shape to protect you. And the only person I trusted at that time was my superior. We didn't have the manpower to assign a guard to be with you twenty-four hours a day." He started to reach out to her, then apparently thought better of it and pulled his hand back. "Not telling you was the only way to keep you safe."

There was nothing that irritated Lauren more than a reasonable argument. Her anger was justified . . . but if she had faced the same choices, would she have done differently?

He struggled up from the couch and retrieved his cane from where he'd leaned it against the bookcase by the kitchen door. "I might have blown all that caution to hell when I contacted you the other night, but there was no other alternative. I doubt that a phone call to you would've sufficed. You wouldn't have paid any attention to the warning."

"What are you talking about?"

His hands absently moved over the shaft of his cane, caressing it. The movement brought to mind the way

Jon's hands used to move over her skin and the pleasure they brought.

"You develop an instinct over years of working in the shadows. That bruise on your wrist combined with what happened today leads me to think someone is using you as bait. Tell me about the accident."

"There's nothing to tell. I'd forgotten to tell the meat-delivery man I needed an extra fifty chickens next Thursday for a banquet. I ran out into the alley, but he was pulling away. When I turned to go back inside, some crates that were stacked by the back door tipped over. I jumped out of the way, but one caught me on the wrist."

Lauren didn't like the ruthless light that entered Jon's eyes. It hit her with the force of an atomic bomb just how dangerous this man was, and how little she knew him. A tiny sliver of fear edged its way into her heart.

"Were there any other accidents?"

"The night before last when I went home, the streetlight in front of my building exploded. I would've been hit by the flying glass if it hadn't been for Mrs. Barn's Yorkshire terrier. Tommy slipped out her apartment door and ran out to greet me. When I bent down to pet Tommy, it put me out of the line of fire."

"And you thought an exploding streetlight was a freak accident? How many other streetlights in London have spontaneously exploded?"

Stated that way, the accident appeared not to be a random event. But then again, when it had happened, Lauren had questioned why a streetlight would just go off like a hand grenade. The incident had shaken her and added to her already jangled nerves.

"Anything else?" he asked.

"No."

"You're sure? Think, Lauren. Anything unusual happen since I appeared in your apartment?"

Lauren remembered the man she'd spotted following her for the past two days. She'd chalked it up to the man working somewhere close to her restaurant.

"What is it? What are you thinking about?"

Her startled gaze flew to his. His smile was gentle.

"I could always read your mind. Remember, you could never hide anything from me."

"Too bad I can't say the same."

His demeanor didn't change, but Lauren felt something inside him harden.

Feeling ashamed of her bitter reply, Lauren said, "Over the last couple of days I've noticed a man who seems to be following me."

"What?" The alarm in his voice set Lauren's nerves on edge. "What man?"

"I noticed him when I got on the Underground two mornings ago. Then I saw him later that day when I went to pick up my cleaning after the lunch rush. I spotted him again on the train the next day."

"Damn."

"There are any number of explanations for me seeing that man. Maybe he's got a job close to my restaurant. Or maybe it was just coincidence."

"It could be a coincidence, but my instincts tell me it isn't just fate."

"Then what is it?"

"I'm not sure, but you can bet your sweet life that guy and the runaway Ford are connected. Now all I have to figure out is who else they're connected to."

Lauren didn't like what he was suggesting, but it had a ring of truth that unnerved her.

* * *

"Your man did what?" Parker James asked, incredulous at what he had just heard.

The other man stared at Parker's outfit, then lifted one eyebrow in disdain. "Do you always dress so atrociously?"

Parker glanced down at his new jeans, snakeskin boots and aqua Western shirt with silver snaps. "Only when I come to see you. And what the hell does that have to do with anything?"

"Nothing."

"Why did you do it?" Parker asked crossly.

"You remember we were going to arrange some accidents for Lauren Michaels?"

Parker remembered them discussing the problem of Lauren seeing their laundry list. "Yes, but they were to be minor accidents."

The man sat back in his chair. "The minor accidents weren't working, so I decided to up the ante. Tiny was instructed not to hurt the lady, but he was to scare the devil out of her."

Parker ran his hands through his hair. "This is unbelievable. What if Tiny had actually hit her?"

Shrugging, the other man answered, "He didn't, but he did discover something very interesting."

"What?"

"Greg Williams walked out of the alley beside the restaurant and pulled Lauren out of danger."

Shock made Parker's knees buckle, and he stumbled into a chair. "What was Greg Williams doing at Lauren's restaurant? He should've been running, trying to hide from the police."

"Exactly my question."

The tension gripping the back of his neck warned Parker that another of his migraines was coming on. He really wasn't cut out for this level of deception, lying to both his government and his friends. He should've never given in to the temptation of the big money waved in front of his face, but he had a weakness for horses and borrowing money from the wrong people. If he had to do it over again, he'd refuse the money. But it was too late; the devil owned him now. "There's something wrong here."

"Oh, I knew there was a reason you were a CIA officer."

The insult hit its mark. Parker wanted to respond in kind, but the man sitting across from him had a nasty, vindictive streak. "What are we going to do?"

"We're going to set up surveillance of both Lauren's apartment and restaurant. I think she'll show up, since she has a passion for that restaurant of hers. Once she does, I want you to go there and see if you can discover where Greg Williams is hiding."

"What if she won't answer the questions?"

The malicious smile that curved the other man's lips made Parker shiver. "I know you'll find a way to get the information out of her. Won't you, Parker?"

"Yeah. I'll find a way."

Jimmy arrived at his apartment a few minutes after nine. Lauren and Jon were sitting on the sofa watching TV when they heard the key in the lock. Jon shot to his feet and started across the room. Before he could reach the door, it swung open. He twisted the shaft of his cane with his left hand, and yanked on the handle with the other. A wicked ten-inch blade emerged from black wood. He pointed the knife at the intruder.

"Jon," Lauren cried, racing across the room. "Don't hurt him. I don't think I could find another Englishman I could teach to make chicken enchiladas."

"It's comforting to know that I'm valued for myself," Jimmy commented crossly.

Lauren flushed and looked down at her hands.

"May I come in?" Jimmy directed his question to the knife-wielding man. "It is, after all, my flat."

Lauren took his arm. "Of course you can come in. Jon was just being cautious."

Calmly Jon reassembled his cane.

"Is he always so cordial?" Jimmy asked as he walked into the living room and set down a large white sack on the coffee table.

"No."

"No?" the Englishman croaked. "You mean he gets worse?"

"No, he doesn't get worse. I mean there are extenuating circumstances that have made Jon a little jumpy."

"A little. Really, Lauren, that's like saying the soccer fans from Liverpool are a little exuberant."

The man across the room chuckled. Jimmy's eyes met his. "So you're a soccer fan?"

"I've been known to bet on a game or two."

Jimmy pointed to the sack. "I brought you something to eat, since I don't have anything in the kitchen here."

"Thanks," Lauren said.

Flopping down on the couch, the young man studied the two people standing side by side. "Who are you?"

"A Good Samaritan."

Jimmy's forehead wrinkled as he studied Jon. Suddenly Jimmy's eyes lit up, and he sprang to his feet. "Ah, Lauren, I need to see you in the kitchen." He clamped his hand around Lauren's wrist and tugged her into the other room. The instant they were alone, he released her. "I know where I saw him." He pointed over his shoulder. "His face is spread all over every London paper. He's accused of murder, Lauren."

Tiredly she sighed. "I know."

"You know?" Jimmy cried incredulously. "Then what are you doing here, in my apartment, with him? Is he holding you against your will?"

"No, I'm not," Jon answered from the doorway.

They whirled to face him.

Jimmy glared at Jon. "Listen, mister, I may not have a fancy cane, but I grew up in the back alleys of Liverpool and know a few nasty tricks."

Lauren clasped Jimmy's arms. "I'm here of my own free will."

"What's the matter with you, Lauren? This is not like you. Did he give you something—a pill, a shot, something in your food?"

"No. The only thing I've eaten since I left the restaurant is some blue cornmeal that I fixed this afternoon."

"I knew it. I knew it. That stuff is no good. I warned you against eating anything that color, but would you listen? No."

"There's nothing wrong with me."

"Right-o. That's why you've run off with a murderer."

Tired of arguing, she laid her hand on Jimmy's arm. "Remember the first time we met? You'd gorged yourself on dinner, then tried to skip out on your bill. But I didn't turn you into the police, did I? Instead, I offered you a job. People said I was a fool to trust you. But I had a feeling about you, Jimmy, that if you were given

a break, you'd make it. I was right. Well, I have the
same feeling about Jon.''

''Jon? The newspaper said the bloke's name was
Greg Williams.''

She waved away the point. ''Whatever. What is important is I have the same feeling about him as I did
about you. If given a break, he'll prove himself.'' As she
argued her point, Lauren realized whoever this man
was, she trusted him on some deep, instinctive level.

Folding his arms over his chest, Jimmy studied the
other man. ''I hope your instinct is right again, because if it isn't, you'll be in trouble up to your little
bum.''

''Why do you say that?'' Jon asked.

''The police came by the restaurant this afternoon,
looking for Lauren. They wanted to question her about
the accident involving the kiosk today. Apparently the
guy who owned it reported the incident.'' His gaze
locked with Lauren's. ''Why didn't you tell me about it
when you called? I felt like an idiot when the police
asked me about the accident.''

''We were pressed for time, Jimmy, and needed to get
out of sight as soon as possible.''

He nodded. ''You have several other problems.''

''What?''

''Apparently all of London, except for me, heard
about your accident. Parker came by. He said he was
worried about you and wanted to check on you.''

Lauren wilted into one of the kitchen chairs. ''How
did he hear about it?''

''I'm wondering the same myself,'' Jon said, pulling
out another chair and sitting.

''And then Donald came into the restaurant tonight.
He asked why you hadn't called him. Apparently you

and he were to have gone to the jewelers today to pick out wedding rings.''

"I forgot," Lauren said, rubbing her temples.

"Donald's a good-natured bloke, but he seemed a bit put out.''

What a mess. Having a husband—or supposed husband—*and* a fiancé was proving to be a problem. "Thanks, Jimmy.''

The young man nodded. "Since this guy isn't too cordial, I'll stay at my girlfriend's flat for a few nights.'' He disappeared into the bedroom, then reappeared several minutes later with a pack slung over his shoulder. Lauren hugged him.

"Thank you, Jimmy. I don't know how I'll ever repay you for this favor.''

"Don't worry, luv, you already have.''

Jimmy reached for the doorknob when Jon's voice stopped him. "You can't tell anyone about us.''

Jimmy threw him a hard look. "I've already covered your backside. I'll continue to do it, but understand I'm doing this for her. Not you, Yank. And if you hurt her, you'll have to answer to me.''

The two men exchanged some hidden message that Lauren was sure was a male thing. Finally Jon nodded, seemingly unoffended by the threat. Jimmy returned the nod, then departed, leaving Lauren to wonder if she would ever understand the male of the species.

Chapter 5

Jon slipped off his sport coat, then checked his watch. It was 9:55. In five minutes he needed to call Diamond in Langley, Virginia. Lauren stood by the door, and from her expression, it was obvious that she was still thinking about the little exchange he'd had with her cook. Jon had to respect the young Englishman. He didn't back away from a fight. Jimmy was very protective of Lauren, and right now she needed all the protection she could get.

"I like your cook. When did you get him?" he asked, trying to ease the tension in her frame.

She leaned back against the smooth wood. "From what you overheard, you can probably guess."

"Humor me and tell me the entire story."

"I met him about six months after *your* reported death."

He had the feeling she was going along with his claims for the sake of finding a way out of this mess.

But he knew she still had doubts, and that was something he couldn't afford.

"Jimmy tried to stiff me for a lunch. It was a welcome relief to know I could still feel something strongly, even if it was just anger. I ran after him and caught him. I gave him the choice of me calling the police or him helping me clean up the lunch mess. He did, then stayed to give me a hand with dinner. And the rest, as they say, is history."

Jon glanced at his watch again. One minute to go. "I have to call my superior, then afterward why don't we eat what Jimmy brought?" Jon hoped she would take the hint and put out the dinner, leaving him alone to make his call.

"All right. I'll dish up the food. But I'll be listening." That keen intellect she possessed showed in her knowing expression. "You can play spy with everyone but me." Snatching up the sack, she marched by him into the kitchen.

Damn, she would've made a good spy. An even better spy master, he thought as he dialed the phone. He waited, listening to the key sequence that diverted the local call to a special number that tapped into the microwave length, skipped across the Atlantic and accessed Diamond's private line.

Again the answering machine clicked on. Where was his boss? It was unlike him not to check messages on this line.

"Diamond, this is Sapphire. As I told you before, Anthony has been murdered, and I've been set up as the prime suspect. Anthony thought he'd discovered the identity of the mole. Apparently the mole figured out he'd been made and killed Anthony. I'm locked out of the embassy and my apartment. I've got no access to our computer files, so I need a copy of the embassy files and a laptop.''

He heard a noise and glanced up to see Lauren standing by the kitchen door, listening to him.

His gaze never left hers as he continued. ''Also, this afternoon someone tried to run Lauren down. She and I are together in hiding.''

Lauren turned and disappeared back into the kitchen.

''I'll check in tomorrow, 1300 hours my time.''

After he hung up, Jon sat staring at the phone. It seemed as if everything in the world was crashing down around him. Anthony dead. Attempts on Lauren's life. Diamond unavailable. What the hell was going on here?

''Are you going to stare at the phone all night or are you going to come and share chicken enchiladas with me?''

''I'm coming.'' He joined her in the kitchen and glanced at the enchiladas covered with a green sauce. ''Ah, the dinner you wanted me to order at the restaurant. You sure you didn't request that Jimmy bring this?''

Doubt appeared in her eyes at his lack of enthusiasm. ''He brought what he had the most of.''

Spanish rice and refried beans accompanied the main dish. A little bit of Texas in the middle of London. With his first bite of the enchilada, Jon knew why Lauren hadn't wanted him to hurt her cook. The man made a mean enchilada.

''You weren't kidding about Jimmy. He's a good cook, Lauren.''

''Don't let him know. Never can tell what Jimmy will ask for.''

Jon laughed, not doubting for a moment the wily Englishman would make the most of any opportunity.

Lauren put her fork down and stared at him as if he had performed some rare and amazing feat.

He felt self-conscious and the tiniest bit lost. He laughed like everyone else. Well, maybe he hadn't in the past few years, but there were reasons for his lack of mirth.

She smiled back at him, a beautiful smile that lighted her eyes and radiated from her like heat from a warm fire. His body instantly responded to her action. The chemistry between Jon and Lauren had always been hot and intense.

"May I ask you a question?" Lauren asked before taking a bite of her rice.

Her voice brought him back to the present with a thud. "Sure."

She pointed to his cane, hooked behind him on the chair back. "Do you really need that or do you only carry it for protection?"

"I need it." He took another bite of his enchilada. The marvelous taste couldn't erase the bitterness of his situation. "My kneecap was shattered in the wreck. I've had several surgeries. I should've spent six more months in physical therapy, but when the new rotation of personnel for the London station approached, our mole got active again. There was a burglary from NATO headquarters of some launch codes. Once they had the codes, we were afraid one of our missiles was going to be targeted." It had frightened everyone in Washington senseless.

"And was one?" Worry darkened her green eyes to almost black.

"There was a try. But since we knew about the missing codes, we beefed up security and prevented the theft. The codes were changed, so even if they had gotten a missile, they would have needed someone who could reprogram the weapon.''

With shaking fingers, she reached for her glass of water. ''Oh.''

''That's not what the guys in Washington said. They were a bit more graphic in their descriptions.''

''So that's why you came to London early?''

''Yeah. It would be natural for me to come in with the new assignments. Unfortunately my knee isn't on a CIA timetable.''

''How bad is it?''

''It's okay if I'm rested. When I get tired, my limp is noticeable and I need the cane for balance. And as you know from experience, if you hit my knee from just the right angle, it folds like a cheap card table. But my superior and I thought it was worth the risk. I wasn't going to be out in the field, slinking around back alleys. I was supposed to be in an office, analyzing data.'' She didn't look comforted by his explanation. ''I have exercises I do every day that supposedly build up my strength and keep the muscles loose.''

He wished he knew what was going on behind those beautiful green eyes of hers. She toyed with the rice on her plate.

''How do you know the mole is in London?''

''We don't, but I know that whoever this guy is, he was in the information pipeline when I went to see the Czech official. I signed out that day on our sheet, stating I was meeting 'Bright Eyes.' That was my code name for the Czech. The communications officer sent a message for me to a neutral third party who set up the meeting.''

Lauren frowned, but from her expression, she was following him.

"The mole could've tapped into the information at any point from the day sheet to the neutral third party. We've tried funneling misinformation along various parts of the line, but so far, none has resurfaced. So my partner and I were trying to track the guy through the crimes."

She rested her fork on her plate and folded her hands in her lap. "Do you enjoy the cloak-and-dagger part of your job?" Her tone and the way she avoided his gaze told him there was a lot more to her question than what she stated. And on a gut level he knew she was asking him if he enjoyed lying to her. Amazingly her unvoiced question was like a knife slicing through him.

"What are you really asking, Lauren?" he asked, careful to keep any emotion out of his voice, but needing to hear her say the sharp words.

Her head jerked up. Her bottom lip trembled, making him want to lean across the table and kiss her soft mouth.

"Why did you join the CIA?"

Coward, he silently replied. So she didn't have the nerve to ask him why he lied. Well, he'd play the game the way she wanted. Maybe he could make her understand why he did what he did.

"I was a senior in college. CIA came recruiting. I wanted to do something for my country, and fighting against communism seemed to me the best way to serve."

"But?" she prompted.

Lauren must have caught the bitterness in his voice. "When you try to outsmart those who play by no rules other than winning, you lose, no matter if you beat them. Lying became second nature. Seeing the ugly side of humanity became common. Youthful ideals are crushed under the weight of the reality of what you have to do.''

He surfaced from the dark images that crowded the halls of his memory. He caught the look of shock and pity in her eyes. For an instant he had let down his guard and allowed her to look into a soul disillusioned and corroded by trickery and deceit. Apparently what she saw shook her to the core. It should have. It scared the hell out of him.

She stood and gathered their plates. As she ran the water for the dishes, Jon noticed the way her shoulders sagged. No matter that his soul was darkened—he didn't want to lose her. He rose, walked to the sink and stood behind her.

''I didn't enjoy lying to you, sweetheart. There was no choice.''

She glanced over her shoulder. ''That's what my mother's ex-husbands said. But there's always a choice.''

His fingers tucked a strand of hair behind her ear. ''No, there isn't. And sometimes when there is, it's a choice between bad and worse.''

She cut off the water and began to wash the plates, trying her hardest to ignore him. He couldn't let her.

''You saved me, Lauren. The little part of my soul that remained untouched, you saved.''

Closing her eyes, she threw her head back. ''Don't do this to me,'' she pleaded softly.

He noticed she never used his name when she was talking to him. That oversight wasn't an accident. She purposely avoided calling him Jon or Greg, no doubt trying to keep her emotional distance from him. He laid his hand on her shoulder, but she jerked away from his touch. ''Don't do what, Lauren?''

"Call up feelings and memories from the past. I can't deal with them. I'm not sure who you are, but I believe you're working for our side. I'll help you, but leave the past buried."

Her words were a challenge, and he wanted to push her into admitting he was Jon. But what he wanted most of all was to lay her down on the kitchen floor, strip the clothes from her shapely body and lose himself in her heat. From her defensive and closed stance, however, he knew it would be like spitting into the wind.

"All right, swe—"

She glared at the endearment.

"Lauren, I'll agree not to bring up the past."

Her body sagged in relief that he wouldn't press her, which perversely angered him.

"But be warned, when this is over and you're safe again, I intend to pursue my claim to your heart." With those last, ringing words, he left the kitchen.

Lauren's hands trembled as she wiped the last plate dry and placed it in the cabinet. The thing that had made her relationship to Jon so special was that beyond the heart-pounding, sizzling attraction they felt for each other, they shared ideas and thoughts. They talked of everything from Milton to politics to the best *masa* to use in tamales. They had shared everything—at least she thought they had shared everything. If he was Jon... Her mind shied away from going down that path. She couldn't deal with wounded feelings now.

Neatly folding the dish towel, she hung it on the rack above the sink. With a deep, fortifying breath, she straightened her shoulders and walked into the living room. A pillow and blanket sat on the couch.

"I thought you could take the bedroom," Jon informed her. "I'll sleep on the couch."

In the rush and excitement of the day, Lauren hadn't considered their sleeping arrangements for the night. Naively she'd thought Jon would hide here and she'd go back to her flat. "I hadn't planned on staying."

He stepped around the ugly plaid monstrosity and into her path. "I'm worried that if you return tonight without someone checking out your apartment or someone to stay with you, whoever arranged the accident with the Ford might try again."

The idea of someone lying in wait for her unnerved her. She considered what happened this afternoon simply an accident, but combined with the other things that had happened since Jon had reappeared in her life, his argument made sense.

"Since you can't accompany me, and you don't trust anyone at the embassy, how do you plan on providing me protection?"

"Once Diamond sends me the disk with the embassy files on it, I might be able to figure out what's going on. If Tony was able to make that deduction, then I should be able to do it, too."

"And how long will that take?"

He shrugged.

"A day? Two? A week?"

"I don't know."

"Jon, I can't spend a week hiding. What will happen to the restaurant? I have obligations. Bills to pay. Employees to see about." She glanced down at her dirty turquoise shirt and Indian print skirt. "And I don't intend to spend a week in this outfit."

His hands cupped her shoulders, his thumbs caressing her collarbone. Their gazes met. It still disoriented her every time she looked into his eyes and saw brown instead of blue. "Lauren, I'm worried about your safety."

"I'll be all right."

"Have you been all right the last three days?"

No, she hadn't, but she wasn't going to admit that to him.

"Listen to me. If anything happened to you—" His expression turned dark and fierce. "All I can think about is that I'm responsible for what happened this afternoon."

She still couldn't accept his words. "No, that can't be possible. There has to be another explanation."

"What?"

"I don't know."

"Then if we don't know, we need to err on the side of caution and assume you're in danger."

She reached up and touched his chin to gain his attention. "How could the mole come to the conclusion that you were Jonathan Michaels when everyone, including the wife, thinks Jonathan Michaels is dead? And even if this person saw you leave my apartment, what would lead him to believe that Greg Williams had anything to do with Jonathan Michaels?"

"My fingerprints may have let the mole know I was alive. Then, the driver of that Ford saw me drag you away to safety. You've been burned, as we'd say in the spy business."

"But—"

His grip on her shoulders tightened. "Between the time I first contacted you and this afternoon, you've had three accidents. That isn't coincidence."

"Stranger things have happened."

He shook his head. "No. In my business nothing is to be taken at face value."

The more he talked, the more he scared her. She tried to shrug out of his grip. He let her. "You know what the trouble is with all you spies?" she asked, trying to shake off the shadows falling across her heart.

His fierce expression softened infinitesimally. "No, but I have the feeling you're going to tell me."

"You're right. You were all hit on the head with the same mallet."

The corner of his mouth twitched. "You could be right," he answered. He laid his palm on her cheek. "I want you to stay here, at least for tonight. When I talk to Diamond again, I'll ask him to send someone in to check out your apartment and see if it's clean. He'll also check to see if it's being watched."

She didn't like the whole situation, but his request was reasonable. "One night."

"We'll discuss it tomorrow."

If he thought he was going to tell her how to run her life and her business, he had a bigger hole in his memory than he knew.

She held up her hand. "One thing."

"What?"

"If Jimmy doesn't have a clean, unused toothbrush, I'm going to make a trip to the corner grocer."

"Lauren—" he started to warn her.

"No. There are some things I will not compromise on." Her mother had this thing about her children brushing their teeth. Lauren had inherited her phobia.

"Why don't you check the bathroom before we have an argument that might not be necessary?"

She flipped on the bathroom light and rummaged through the shelf above the sink, the cabinet under the sink and the towel cabinet. Nothing. When she walked back into the living room, Jon was holding up a boxed, new toothbrush.

"Where did you get that?"

"In the kitchen. I thought I remembered seeing one when we searched the cabinets earlier." He placed it in her palm. His fingers caressed the back of her hand. The soft, provocative touch made her want to feel his fingers on her skin again.

"When I was searching for this, I remembered the time on our honeymoon when you dropped your toothbrush in the toilet. There we were in the middle of the night, pounding on Mr. McGee's door, begging him to open up his store."

Lauren's hand convulsively closed around the toothbrush she held, crushing the box. How did he know about that incident? She hadn't ever told anyone about that. The memory of what happened after she bought the toothbrush exploded in her brain.

His intense gaze made her breathing shaky and her stomach tremble. This man wanted her. And she, in spite of these unbelievable circumstances straight out of a bad movie, wanted him. Right here, right now on the ugly plaid sofa.

Suddenly she remembered Donald, to whom she was still engaged. No matter who the man standing before her was, she couldn't make love to him while still engaged to another man. It was obvious to her that she had to tell Donald she couldn't marry him.

"If I stay here, you'll have to have another bowl of blue cornmeal for breakfast tomorrow."

"I'd rather dodge bullets than eat that stuff again. But if eating it will keep you safe, I'll eat it for the next three weeks, morning, noon and night."

Somehow the light exchange she intended turned poignant, almost beyond bearing. He leaned down and lightly kissed her.

"Good night, sweetheart."

Lauren turned and hurried back into the bathroom before she broke into tears.

Jon breathed a huge sigh of relief as the door to the bathroom closed. Lauren had scared him spitless when she'd stated she wanted to go back to her apartment tonight. No matter what she thought, what had happened this afternoon had been no accident. He felt it in his bones. Lauren's accidents were part of a plan. What he needed to figure out was what was the plan and who was behind it.

He heard the water of the shower come on and smiled to himself. Not only was it obvious Lauren had a fixation about brushing her teeth, but he'd guess she also had this thing about showering daily. He was lucky he'd run across that toothbrush incident in her diary the other day, refreshing his memory. Knowing about it undercut doubts she had about him.

Quit thinking about the woman in the shower, he sternly told himself. Instead of wasting his time on far-fetched fantasies, he needed to talk to Diamond. After dialing, he waited for his boss to pick up the phone. The answering machine clicked on.

"Diamond, I need for you to pull someone and have them check Lauren's apartment and see if it's under surveillance or if someone is there waiting for her.

Lauren has the idea she wants to go back home." He relayed the accidents that had occurred to Lauren, then hung up.

What was going on here and where was Diamond? he wondered with growing concern. He wiped his hand over his face. His beard felt rough under his palm, and as soon as Lauren vacated the bathroom, he would see if Jimmy had a razor. His beard had to go. If he was clean shaven, it might help disguise him when he ventured out of this apartment.

He pulled his shirt out of his pants and began to unbutton it. The bathroom door opened, and his fingers froze over the last button. Lauren was wrapped in a towel that barely covered her from breasts to hips.

"Uh..." She blushed. "Apparently Jimmy doesn't own a robe, and I washed my shirt and underclothes."

He nodded, but he couldn't tear his gaze away from the generous amount of bosom overflowing the top of the towel.

"The bathroom is yours," she said lamely, moving toward the bedroom. With each step she took, the edges of the towel parted, giving him a good view of her shapely hip.

His body instantly responded to the sight. He wanted to moan with the pain of his arousal. Of course, why should he be surprised by his body's reaction? The woman was beautiful. Any man with warm blood flowing in his veins would have the same reaction.

When the door to the bedroom closed behind her, Jon's head rolled forward with relief. He didn't know how long he would be able to endure this torture of being so close to Lauren and not give in to the urge to make love to her.

He stripped off his shirt, laid it on the back of the couch and walked into the bathroom. The first things he saw were her bra and panties hanging over the towel rack. He froze and swallowed hard. Unable to help himself, his fingers ran over the champagne-colored lace of her bra.

"Don't do this to yourself," he muttered.

The Stasi, the East German secret police, couldn't have invented a more exquisite torment than him seeing these things and imagining himself taking them off of the owner.

He turned and saw the safety razor on the shelf above the sink. A box of new blades was beside the razor. After changing the blade, he went into the living room to look for a pair of scissors. He found them in the kitchen, then returned to the bathroom to cut his beard close enough that he could shave.

With his beard and mustache, it had been relatively easy to fool the people at the embassy into believing he was Greg Williams. The cover story put out was that he'd been hurt in a car accident a few miles away from CIA headquarters in Langley, Virginia, which explained his need of a cane. But Lauren was another story. Could he make her believe he was Jon when he tried so hard to make everyone else believe he was Greg?

He set the scissors aside and began to lather his face. Lauren was one smart lady. Sometimes he didn't feel he would ever convince her he was Jon. But he was going to try his damnedest.

His gaze drifted to Lauren's underthings hanging on the towel rack. His attention distracted, he cut his cheek. Cursing, he pressed his finger to the bleeding wound. Well, why was he surprised? Lauren had been a distraction for him since the moment he'd met her. And that probably would be his downfall.

Chapter 6

She couldn't sleep—not with a thousand conflicting emotions clogging her head like cars in rush-hour traffic. She flipped onto her back and stared at the ceiling. Jimmy's appearance tonight had forced her to face some rather uncomfortable realities. She trusted the man asleep in the other room who claimed to be her husband. The more time she spent with him, the more confident she became that her trust in him was justified. The memories that spilled from his mouth, the manner in which he talked with her, the way his eyes focused on some imaginary point when he was thinking were all pieces to a puzzle that was slowly filling in before her eyes.

If he truly was Jon—no, she wouldn't let herself even consider that. And yet how had he known about the intimate details of their lovemaking? How did he know about the toothbrush?

Her quivering insides refused to calm down. There was something odd or slightly off in this whole situation. Rather like a yankee from Brooklyn telling you how to cook collard greens and grits—the pieces didn't fit.

It had taken three years of hard work to put her life back together again. She'd been devastated by Jon's death. They'd been married a little less than a year when the news came of his car accident in France. She had locked herself in her apartment and had not come out for six weeks.

At first she couldn't stand to be at work. The place was filled with memories of Jon—of how he'd come into the restaurant for lunch for three weeks straight before he asked her out. How he'd proposed in the kitchen over a plate of refried beans and rice. How they stole time in her little office to be together.

Every day had been a battle. Some days she couldn't work the entire day. Others, she went home in tears. Then one day about six months after Jon's reported death Jimmy showed up and pulled his "let's leave without paying" routine. He kept her thoughts off her sorrow and on teaching him to cook. About the same time, she met Donald at a restaurant convention in Liverpool. She liked him, and he had eased the loneliness eating away at her heart. They talked the ins and outs of the restaurant business with ease. So when Donald proposed, Lauren had accepted without questioning her feelings too closely.

Now, unfortunately, she had to pull back the protective layer she'd wrapped herself in and take a hard look at what she felt for Donald.

What kind of a woman would run off with a stranger who claimed to be her dead husband and leave her perfectly healthy fiancé waiting to pick out their weddings rings? What kind of woman would be attracted to said stranger more than to her fiancé? And what kind of woman would be stirred more by a stranger's touch than her fiancé's?

A woman who is not in love with her fiancé, her conscience whispered.

As if punched in the stomach, she bolted into a sitting position. Sometimes true revelation was the pits. Kind of like finding out the cat that ran under your car was a skunk.

She wrapped her arms around her legs and rested her chin on her knees.

Friendship is a good basis for a marriage, she sternly told herself.

Oh, yeah, a little voice answered. *You can play chess in friendly silence while you shrivel up inside and resemble a prune like your old Aunt Mildred.*

Lauren shivered. Her aunt was a legend in her family. It was said she made her husband come to dinner in a coat and tie and called him Mr. Atwood until the day he died. Attila the Hun had a lighter touch than Aunt Milly. All the children in her family were threatened with time at Aunt Milly's house if they misbehaved at family gatherings.

Did she want to end up like Aunt Milly? A sob caught in her throat.

The bedroom door flew open. Jon stood there, and in the soft moonlight that filled the room she could see the blade of his cane in his left hand. "Lauren? Are you all right?"

Startled, she sat up straight, causing the sheet to fall to her waist. She felt Jon's gaze narrow to her chest. Snatching the sheet back, she tucked it under her arms.

"Yes," she choked. "I couldn't sleep. I'm sorry I woke you."

He replaced the blade into his cane, then took a step forward, bringing his face into the stream of moonlight.

Lauren stared at his naked cheeks and jaw. "You shaved."

His hand skimmed over his smooth chin. "Yeah. Now I'm not as easily recognized."

She nodded.

"You want some tea?" he asked.

Lauren was well aware of her nakedness beneath the sheet. "Uh..."

He disappeared, then reappeared with his shirt and handed it to her. "Here, wear this."

She peeked at his bare chest lightly covered with hair. Aunt Milly would never approve.

Lauren felt self-conscious dressing in front of him. He must have read her discomfort and turned his back. She hurriedly slipped out of bed and into the shirt. The sleeves hung past her fingertips, and the tails ended above her knees.

"Let's hope Jimmy has some tea in this flat," she said, trying to ignore the feel of the fabric against her skin. She began to roll up the sleeves.

He turned. One black brow arched, disappearing under the fall of his hair. "Are you kidding me? Whoever heard of an Englishman who didn't have tea in his house?"

A laugh escaped her mouth. "I guess you're right."

They found a half-empty tin of Earl Grey in a cabinet with the sugar bowl and teacups. Lauren tried to keep her eyes off the wide expanse of Jon's chest as he prepared the tea, but her eyes kept returning to the well-

muscled torso and arms that were marked with dozens
of scars.

"Do I look that bad?"

She jumped, flushing guiltily. "No."

"Then what?"

"The scars. Are they from the accident?"

An arctic coldness entered his eyes. "Yes."

It occurred to her at that moment that he had his
contacts out and his eyes were Jon's familiar blue. With
his entire face revealed, she could see his high cheek-
bones and strong chin. The scar that ran from his left
temple disappeared under his jawbone. But as she gazed
at his face, some memory stirred to life in her.

He placed the teapot on the table, startling her out of
her musings. Lauren poured while Jon retrieved the
sugar and cream. Cream? She didn't take cream in her
tea, and neither did the real Jon.

"Do you still take your tea without cream?" Jon
asked.

"Yes."

He poured a generous amount into his cup. "Before
the accident I couldn't stand cream in my tea, but a
nurse at the clinic in Bath, where I recovered, who
looked like she played fullback for the New York Gi-
ants, always served me tea with cream and no one dared
argue with her. Now tea tastes strange without it."

He was an excellent liar. She'd seen him in action, up
close and personal. Was he lying now? Just as she was
convinced this man was Jon, some little thing would
pop up, pointing to the possibility he wasn't. It was
confusing, tiring and frustrating.

"Why couldn't you sleep?" he asked softly.

The 64,000-dollar question. *Well, you see, I have the
hots for you and it bothers me, since I'm engaged to*

another man and I don't know if you're my dead husband or a raving lunatic. She shook her head. That answer would never do. Leaning back in her chair, she skimmed her fingers around the lip of her cup. "My life's been turned upside down and inside out, and you ask me why I can't sleep?"

"Yeah, I guess you're right. It's not every day that a car tries to run you down."

She glanced down at the shirt she wore—his shirt—then pushed the rolled-up sleeves past her elbows. "I still believe that was an accident."

"It wasn't."

From the set of his chin and the hardness of his eyes, she knew she wouldn't convince him otherwise. "One thing's been bothering me."

"Only one thing?" he returned, his face lighting with mischief.

"A thousand and one things, really, but this one I think you can answer."

"Shoot."

They stared at each other for several seconds before bursting into laughter.

"How did you happen to be there today, just at the right time to save me from that cab?"

"Still doubting me?" he countered.

"Well, you have to admit that it was a suspicious coincidence. Your timing was a little too perfect."

"No coincidence. I'd gone to the restaurant to explain about Tony before I disappeared. I saw you walking back to the restaurant, then stop to read the newspaper. The Ford wasn't hard to spot."

"Oh."

"Mind if I ask you a question?" he asked.

"Turnabout is fair play. What do you want to know?"

He picked up her left hand in his and carefully examined her fingers. "If you and Donald have already had an engagement party, why aren't you wearing an engagement ring? I would think a man of his social status would give his fiancée a ring."

Lauren pulled her hand free. "He did, but it was too big. That's one of the reasons we were going to the jewelers today, to pick it up."

He studied her, but his expression gave away nothing of what he was thinking, making Lauren very nervous. "Do you still have the wedding ring I gave you?"

"It's been three years since you died."

"I didn't ask why you don't wear it. I only wondered if you still had it."

Unable to endure his scrutiny any longer, she took her empty cup and set it in the sink. He joined her. The heat from his body wrapped around her, drawing her to him. He reached in front of her to place his cup next to hers. She looked over her shoulder, and their eyes met and locked. Like lightning arcing from one cloud to another, a charged current passed between them. He reached for her, turned her around and pulled her against his naked chest.

"Do you still have it?"

The feel of his skin against her cheek was as joyful as the first warm winds of spring. "Yes, I have it."

Without realizing it, she slipped her arms around his waist and lifted her face to his. His warm, moist lips covered hers, igniting a fire storm in her veins. He nudged her mouth, seeking entrance to the treasures beyond. She yielded, and the burning arrow of pleasure that pierced her body nearly reduced her to a pile of ashes at his feet.

Her hands skimmed up his spine and over the broad muscles of his back. His smooth skin was interrupted periodically by thin crisscrossing ridges.

Reality intruded and she drew back.

His passion-glazed eyes met hers, and she read in their smoldering depths the question of why she pulled away.

"I'm sorry," she whispered, looking down at her hands.

His fingers under her chin forced her gaze back to his. "Why are you sorry?" he asked bitterly. "Sorry you enjoyed it? Or sorry you returned my kiss? Or sorry you'll deny us both?"

"You have no right."

"I'm your husband."

Like a volcanic eruption, anger shot up through her. "So you say. But I'm not sure who you really are. Even if you are Jon, too much has happened for me to hop into bed with you without a word of protest."

She whirled and took three steps, then turned back. "Besides, I have a fiancé, and no matter what you think of me, I won't sleep with you before I sever my relationship with him. I don't jump ship midstream. *I* at least give those I love some closure."

Immediately she realized it was the wrong thing to say. His blue eyes flared with a burning light, and his facial muscles turned to stone. With one step he closed the distance between them.

"Do you love him?"

She wanted to lie, to wound him. But her gaze drifted to the scars on his chest, and she knew she couldn't do that, no matter what he had done.

"I like him."

"But do you *love* him?"

"Love's overrated."

Something flickered in his eyes. Pain, loss, regret? "Now who's the liar?"

She opened her mouth to refute his statement, but after seeing the dark warning in his expression, her jaw snapped shut before she uttered a word.

"You always were a smart lady."

"Urrgh!" She tried to stomp away, but he caught her wrist.

He studied her, then reached out and tucked a long strand of hair behind her ear. His thumb brushed over her bottom lip. Once. Twice. Lauren thought all the air in the room had been sucked out, because she couldn't catch her breath.

"One of these days you'll trust me enough to come to me on your own," he told her, his voice low and rough with need. "I hope that day will be soon."

She glared at him.

"Tell me this, Lauren. Why would I claim to be Jon? What benefit is it to me? I've got nothing to gain except getting my wife back."

He released her wrist, and she rushed into the bedroom, slamming the door behind her. She walked to the window and stared out into the street. His question rolled through her mind like thunder on a spring night. What did he have to gain? Her flat? Her cranky, ancient MG? Her restaurant? He didn't seem like the kind of man interested in spending his life managing foodstuffs and waiters.

Then what?

Had Jon left her anything that might be of value? No, he had only left clothes and a few books.

Could he be after Donald, trying to get to him through her? That made no sense.

Wrapping her arms around her waist, she sat on the bed. She couldn't answer his question. But this much she knew. She was drawn to this man, like a june bug was attracted to the light. When she was growing up in Kaufman, Texas, she could remember lying in bed at night during the hot summer listening to the bug's futile attempt to get inside to the hall light. It mindlessly hurled itself against the screens until it died of exhaustion or found a hole in the wire mesh.

What would be her fate? Would she be able to penetrate the lies and half truths that surrounded the man calling himself Jonathan Michaels and find the truth? Or would she die trying? It was a less than comforting analogy.

Jon sat on the sofa, his elbows resting on his knees, his head cradled in his hands. Well, he certainly had blown it with Lauren. With his hormones driving him, he had pushed her too hard, too fast. He couldn't afford to do that again. He needed to win her trust, not alienate her. And yet whenever he was close to her, his mind seemed to go on hold and his body took over. She evoked feelings in him that were dangerous, that drew his thoughts away from the problem of finding the mole, drew him to the desire to taste her lips.

Every time he thought about her being engaged, it made him crazy. He was afraid if he ever met Donald Blake face-to-face, he'd feed the Englishman a knuckle sandwich.

He sighed and stretched out on the couch. His bad knee was throbbing, telling him that he'd been on it too long. Because of the injury, he could no longer serve as a case officer, recruiting foreign nationals to gather information. Nor could he be sent into a foreign country as a singleton as he had been in the past. He was now desk bound.

But if he were honest with himself, he wasn't terribly disappointed. He was tired of the lies, tired of always trying to discern people's motives, tired of always watching his back. That's why Lauren meant so much to him. What you saw was what you got. Pretty and sassy. And smart. And if he didn't watch it, he was going to blow this opportunity all to hell. He couldn't afford to do that. Too much rested on Lauren believing he was her husband.

Lauren glanced in the bathroom mirror one last time. Her hair was in a tight braid, and she was dressed in her wrinkled blouse and skirt. She looked as if she'd slept in her clothes, but at least they were clean. Her face was devoid of any makeup, and there were dark circles under her eyes. Well, there was no help for it. She hadn't slept and she looked like it.

She was mad, having wrestled with her doubts and attraction to Jon all night. She grabbed his shirt, opened the bathroom door and walked into the living room. Jon sat on the couch, his elbows resting on his knees, his shoulders hunched. She could see his back and the numerous scars that crisscrossed it. Her heart ached for him. No matter who he was, the man had suffered through a tremendous amount of pain. She remembered the scars on his legs and the ugly red mass around his injured knee.

"Good morning," he said, his voice low and rough.

That was something else about this man that disturbed Lauren. The gravelly quality was unlike Jon's, but it was dark and sensual and always evoked dangerous emotions in her.

He pointed to the shirt in her hand. "Are you returning that?"

Color flooded her cheeks. She felt as though she was ten again with a crush on eleven-year-old Mickey-Bob Shelton. She'd been so enamored with the skinny boy that she'd managed to walk into the cafeteria wall at school while trying to catch his attention. She now felt the same feeling of embarrassment with the same painful clarity.

She shoved the shirt at him. An amused smile curved his lips as he took it from her hand. Like stepping in front of a blast furnace, the heat of his smile warmed Lauren from head to foot. Her stomach seemed to do a somersault, and she knew that if she spent another second staring into his handsome face, she was going to hop over the sofa and kiss him. Her reaction further fed her irritation.

"I'm going to fix blue cornmeal. Do you want some?"

"Do I have a choice?" Laughter laced his words.

She rested her fists on her hips. "Yes or no."

"Yes."

She marched into the kitchen without a backward glance and started breakfast. As she cooked the mush, Lauren came to the conclusion she was going to have to get out of this flat if she had any hope of surviving Jon's magnetic pull on her will. Her heart felt like a pretzel, twisted and pulled around on itself, and she couldn't seem to regain any of the sense of balance or objectivity she needed to make a decent judgment.

Jon limped into the room several minutes later, leaning heavily on his cane. His hair was wet, his shirt on, and the look in his eyes utterly weary. The sight aroused her sympathy and made her want to comfort him. In this situation those were bad impulses.

"Breakfast is ready," she announced unnecessarily.

He frowned at the bowls of cereal on the table.

"It was your choice," she reminded him. "Last night I volunteered to get eggs and muffins, but you nixed the idea."

"Don't remind me."

As they ate, she glanced at his cane. His limp was very pronounced this morning.

"I told you, my limp is worse when I'm tired."

Her gaze flew to his, and her cheeks heated with embarrassment. He had read her mind with amazing accuracy.

"And are you wondering what kept me awake most of the night?"

She didn't want to hear.

He leaned across the table and whispered, "You."

She jerked back in her chair. The conversation was drifting down a dangerous avenue. She wanted to redirect the focus. "Do you think your, uh, disability will hamper your—"

"Do you mean does my limp blow my spying days to hell?"

"Kinda."

He laughed, but there was no humor in the sound. "Not completely. I can still sit behind a desk and do analysis, but my days in the field are finished."

She swallowed a spoonful of her cereal, then asked, "Do you regret it?"

He picked up his cup of tea and gazed into the golden liquid. "I don't know. I know I'm bitter that I didn't have the choice of when to quit. And now I'm determined to find the bastard who betrayed me and killed Tony."

The rest of the meal passed in silence. Lauren gathered the bowls and put them in the sink. She poured them both a second cup of tea, mentally preparing herself for the argument she was going to precipitate.

"I'm going in to work today," she said, picking up her cup.

His gaze locked with hers. He hadn't put in the brown contacts this morning. It made her crazy to gaze into his blue eyes. It was one less barrier to keep her sane. And one more reason to escape the small confines of these four walls.

"You promised to stay until I checked if it was safe for you—"

"To go to my apartment. I said nothing about work."

"You're being legalistic."

"You got it. I'll keep to the letter of my promise."

"But not the spirit."

"From you, that's quite a statement."

He paled as the barb hit its mark. Stumbling to his feet, he said, "Dammit, Lauren, you're just being pig-headed."

She leapt up. "I'd say that makes two of us."

"My only concern is you."

She couldn't argue with his concern, but she was desperate to escape his presence. So she said nothing but raised her chin in silent determination.

He sighed and shook his head. "At least stay until I talk to my superior."

"I can't. I'll be safe at the restaurant."

He grabbed her wrist, showing her the purple-and-yellow bruise. "Like you were when this happened?"

"Listen to me. If you think I'm going to stay in this flat all day long, sitting on my rear doing nothing, while my restaurant is unattended, then you've seriously miscalculated. That hole in your memory is bigger than you think."

She tried to yank her arm free, but he wouldn't release her. He attempted to intimidate her with his stare, but she returned his glare.

"If I have to wrestle you," she told him, "I will. And if you remember, the last time we went a round, I won."

His mouth twitched at the corners, then he released her and stepped aside. She strode across the flat to the front door. As she opened it, she thought she heard him say, in an intimate whisper, "Be careful."

Jon stood back from the window and watched as Lauren walked down the street toward the Underground station. He certainly had handled her with a suave and elegant manner, much like a hog caller yelling at swine. He definitely was losing his touch.

His stomach knotted with tension. Although he had no concrete proof, his gut instinct was screaming at him that there was an unseen threat against Lauren. Why wouldn't she believe him that her life was in danger?

Could it be that you've lied to her more than you've told her the truth since you've known her? his conscience whispered.

He walked away from the window and collapsed onto the couch. And what could he do to protect her? Run down the street to catch her and force her back to the safety of Jimmy's place? Yeah, right. A toddler could outrun him. And even if he could catch up with her, Lauren wouldn't come quietly back.

So what could he have done?

Nothing. Absolutely nothing. And that's what had him so frustrated. He rubbed his throbbing temples as he faced the ugly truth of this situation. His lies were catching up to him.

And unfortunately Lauren might be the one who paid for his sins.

Halfway to the restaurant, Lauren decided that she looked too rumpled and felt too messy to step into Santa Fe Station. She'd worked too hard over the past few years to show up this shabby. She needed to change clothes. Jon would probably have a fit if he knew she was going to her flat, but what he didn't know wouldn't hurt him. Besides, the man had lied so often to her, how did she know he hadn't lied this time, too?

Her building looked fine, and everything appeared normal. Even the streetlight that had blown up had been replaced.

As she walked down the hallway to her flat, her neighbor Cassie emerged from hers.

"My, my, what happened to you? And where have you been all night?" A light sparked in Cassie's eyes. "You finally spent the night with Donald. Congratulations."

The furthest thing from Lauren's mind was sleeping with her fiancé. She opened her mouth to deny the accusation, then shut it. Better Cassie think she'd been with Donald than with another man.

Cassie hugged her. "It's about time. Well, I'd love to chat, but I'm late for work." She hurried down the hall. "Oh," she called, pausing at the building's door, "Parker James came by last night looking for you, luv. He was worried about you. You best ought to give the gent a call."

"Terrific," Lauren grumbled as she let herself in her apartment.

There was an odd feeling to the silent rooms. She tried to shake off the feeling, telling herself that it was a guilty conscience plaguing her. Nevertheless, Lauren walked through each room, searching for clues that someone had been there. Nothing seemed out of place. And yet she had this creepy feeling someone had been inside her flat.

After changing and applying makeup, she raced out of her place and barreled into a little old lady who was in the hall.

"Excuse me," Lauren said, steadying the woman.

"Certainly."

As Lauren hurried outside, she wondered who the woman was there to see, because she didn't live in the building.

Chapter 7

Lauren smiled at the young detective. After leaving her flat, she'd gone straight to the police station and patiently answered all the queries the police had concerning the hit-and-run. "If you don't have any more questions, I do need to get to my restaurant."

"If I do, I'll ring you." He offered his hand, and she shook it. "My thanks, Mrs. Michaels, for your cooperation."

Mrs. Michaels. Hearing that name was like being hit in the side of the head with a frying pan. No one had called her "Mrs." in nearly three years.

"Are you all right, madam?"

She swallowed around the large lump in her throat. "Yes."

Lauren stood and tried to keep her walk to an easy stride until she hit the front door of the police station. Then she ran mindlessly to the end of the block. At the curb she stopped. Sucking in a deep breath, she tried to calm her racing heart.

What was wrong with her? Nothing that getting rid of a spy wouldn't cure.

She winced, recalling the heated words she and Jon had exchanged earlier.

The light changed, and she was able to cross the busy street. Stuck at Jimmy's, what good was she to either herself or Jon? By carrying on her normal daily routine, she felt that somehow, something would turn up.

A satisfying feeling washed over her when her restaurant came into view. The instant she walked inside, Jimmy grabbed her by the arm.

"There's something you need to see in your office," he said. From his intensity she guessed that Jimmy's statement was simply an excuse to talk to her privately.

He followed her through the dining area and kitchen to her little corner room. After closing the door, he asked, "Are you all right?"

"Yes."

He frowned. "Well, I didn't like the bloke you hid in my flat."

"You're just holding a grudge because he pulled a knife on you."

"Funny thing, I have me a nasty disposition when I'm looking at the wrong end of a dagger."

Lauren waved away his comment.

"Have you seen the newspaper today?" Jimmy pressed. "It has a long story about that man. He's dangerous. I worry about you, Lauren."

"I'll admit that things look bad for Jon. But I am not in any danger."

Jimmy grunted his disagreement.

"Has anything happened so far today that I need to know about?"

"Let's see." Jimmy held out his hand and began to count off the things. "Donald phoned. You must call, his orders. Parker James also rang you. The meat-delivery man didn't bring all the chickens you ordered. And the Fazeo brothers didn't deliver the vegetables this morning. But never fear, I already called the gents and set them right. I'm expecting them to show up at any moment."

Lauren wilted into her chair. She'd been gone only half a day. What would've happened if she'd let Jon talk her into staying away today? "Where do I start?"

Jimmy grabbed the phone and handed her the receiver. "Ring Donald." He strode to the door.

"Jimmy."

He paused.

"Thanks for holding down the fort."

He nodded, then left.

Lauren dialed Donald's number and discovered he wasn't in his office. "Tell him to call me when he gets in," she told his secretary. "I'm at work."

That was the high point of her day. The Fazeo brothers never showed with the veggies, and she didn't have enough chickens to make it through the evening meal. Finally, in desperation, Lauren called Marshall Blake, her soon-to-be ex-future-father-in-law.

"Marshall, I'm in desperate straits. My suppliers have decided to take an unannounced vacation. Can you help me out with some vegetables and chickens?"

"Anything for you. Tell me what you need, and I'll have the warehouse pull the stuff and send it right over."

"You're a lifesaver."

"Have you talked to Donald today? He was quite upset about you missing your appointment with the jeweler yesterday." Although the tone of his voice was still pleasant, Lauren heard the rebuke in his words. "The man had another opening day after tomorrow. Donald booked it."

She noted the new time on her blotter, then shook her head. There were no rings in her future—at least no rings bought for and by Donald. "I'm sorry about the mix-up. But right now I've got a couple of emergencies here to tend to. I'll tell you all about what happened yesterday later. Thanks for all your help."

She hung up quickly. A commotion in the kitchen caught her attention. Instantly she charged out of her office, only to come to a dead stop when she saw Parker James standing inside the kitchen door. He was staring down at the tray of food he'd knocked out of a waiter's hands.

"I'm terribly sorry, Lauren," Parker said, stepping around the mess. "I'll be happy to pay for the damages."

The waiter glared up at Parker. Lauren ushered Parker back into the dining room before anything else could be said.

She settled Parker into a corner table, then grabbed two glasses with ice and poured tea into them.

"I heard about your near miss yesterday," Parker began. "I was twice as worried when I couldn't find you yesterday afternoon or at your flat last night. Are you okay, Lauren?"

This time Lauren found Parker's concern annoying and presumptuous. Think fast, she told herself, and come up with a good excuse for being gone as long as she was. Resting her elbows on the table, she leaned forward. "Can you keep a secret?"

He jerked back as if she'd slapped him. It took a moment for him to compose his features. "You know I can."

"After that near miss, I was pretty shaken up. When you come that close to dead, you reevaluate your life."

"That's understandable."

"Well, there's this little shop in Grasmere that had the most beautiful lavender wool sweater and skirt. I saw it last month when I was there on vacation. They were an expensive set, and I talked myself out of buying them." She ran her fingers around the rim of her glass. "But after yesterday I decided life was too short to deny myself all pleasure, so I took the train to Carlisle, then rented a car and drove to Grasmere. I bought the outfit, then spent the night at a bed and breakfast. I came back this morning."

The lie rolled easily off her tongue. Maybe being around the man who claimed to be Jon was wearing off on her, and she was becoming an expert liar.

Lauren held her breath, waiting to see if Parker would swallow her story. He knew that sometimes when she was upset, she would take several hours and shop. She'd done it in the past.

"Lauren, you should've told someone. If not me, then someone here at your restaurant. I was very worried when you just vanished."

Fighting to suppress her irritation, she smiled. "You're right. Next time I decide to run off to the Lake District, I'll invite you along."

From his expression, Parker didn't quite know what to make of her comment. Lauren wanted to bite her tongue for snapping out the facetious reply.

"Did you get the name of the man who pulled you to safety? I mean, I'm sure the police would like to honor him for being such a courageous fellow."

What was wrong with this picture? Something was out of kilter. Lauren leaned back in her chair. "How did you know about that?"

"Why, I talked to the owner of the newsstand out front. After all, I was very concerned. The owner said the man seemed to come from out of nowhere to pluck you out of danger."

She wasn't about to ID Jon to Parker. "I was pretty upset and by the time I caught my breath, he'd disappeared. I wasn't even able to thank him." Parker didn't look convinced. She shrugged. "I guess he was a Good Samaritan and wanted no reward."

He looked even less pleased with her answer.

It was foolish to sit here and continue to make up excuses. Lauren stood and plastered a pleasant—or what she hoped was a pleasant—smile on her face. "Thank you for being such a good friend, Parker. I'm fine and I appreciate your concern."

He looked as if he wanted to say more. Instead, he simply nodded. "Well, I need to get back to the embassy."

About time, she silently said.

She escorted him to the front door and waved goodbye. When she walked back inside, her stomach clenched. She definitely was not cut out to be a superghost or spook or whatever they were called. If she didn't have an ulcer by the end of the day, she certainly would be well on her way to one. She hurried to the kitchen and grabbed a glass of buttermilk and downed the contents, knowing it would ease the ache in her stomach.

One of the waiters opened the kitchen door and leaned in. "Lauren, there's a man out front with a parcel for you.

Odd, she hadn't ordered anything. She followed the waiter out front. After signing for the package, Lauren carefully observed how it was addressed—her name and the street address of her restaurant. The edges of the label were banded with thick black lines except where they met at the left bottom corner. There was a diamond imprinted. Normally she wouldn't have paid any attention to the label, but that small diamond gave her hope that this might be from Jon's boss.

She rushed back to her office and opened the parcel. Inside she found a laptop, a box of disks and a letter addressed to her. Ripping the envelope open, she scanned the page: "Lauren, I'm sending this to you since you know where our mutual friend is. Diamond."

Well, at least Jon's boss had gotten his messages. She needed to get this information to Jon immediately. Folding the outside wrapping into a small square, she placed it and the box of disks in her purse, then grabbed the laptop.

Jimmy looked up when she emerged from her office.

"I have an errand to run," she quietly told him. "I'll be back in about forty-five minutes."

He nodded.

Lauren hurried out of the kitchen door into the alley. The Blake Catering truck had just turned into the alley. Remembering yesterday when Jon used the office building next to the restaurant to aid their getaway, Lauren walked around the corner and slipped into the side door. The halls were deserted, for which she was thankful. Exiting on the next street, she hailed a cab.

She took it halfway, then switched cabs. The second taxi dropped her off one street north of her destination. She then walked the rest of the distance. The best she could tell, no one had followed her.

Lightly she knocked on number 12, Jimmy's flat. "Jon, it's Lauren," she said softly through the wood.

The shiny black door swung open, but Lauren didn't see anyone. "Come inside," Jon's voice instructed. She stepped inside, and the door closed behind her, causing her to jump. Jon stood by the door hinges, the dagger of his cane in one hand, the base in the other.

"You really need to work on your social skills, Jon."

He shrugged and reassembled the weapon. "It's a hazard of the profession."

Lauren set the laptop on the coffee table.

He frowned at the blue sweater and loose black skirt she wore.

"Did you go to your apartment?"

Of all the men in the world who couldn't remember from one minute to the next what their wives or girlfriends had on, she got the one who did. "Uh..."

His hand swept up and down her body. "You've changed since leaving."

She picked at the neck of her sweater. "I needed something else to wear. The things I had on looked like I slept in them, so I went to my flat and changed."

Jon moved toward her. She wanted to retreat from the fury burning in his blue eyes, but she was already standing with her legs against the coffee table.

Seizing her upper arms, he brought her face close to his. "You did an extremely foolish thing, Lauren. You placed yourself in danger unnecessarily. What if, while you were changing, the driver of that Ford broke into your apartment and kidnapped or—even worse—killed you?''

She tried to shrug off his hands, but he refused to release her. ''Nothing happened. I'm fine.''

He drew in a deep breath as if steadying himself. ''But it could've. Don't you understand these people are fighting for their lives? They'd think nothing of eliminating you. And that's something I couldn't have endured.'' He released his hold and slid his hands over her shoulders and neck to frame her face. His thumb brushed her bottom lip, caressing the petal smoothness. Slowly, his gaze never leaving her mouth, he lowered his head until their lips touched. She tasted of honey and spice. A taste he'd never forget.

She groaned and he slipped his tongue into her mouth. He felt his control dissolving as she returned his ardor. Wrapping his arms around her waist, he drew her close. Her wobbly legs buckled, and she leaned into him. Suddenly, with her weight resting on his right side, his bad knee gave out under the added pressure, and they tumbled to the floor.

Sprawled on top of him, Lauren shook her head and propped her elbows on his chest. ''You certainly know how to sweep a girl off her feet.''

His face was blank, then he burst into laughter. ''You're one in a million. A lady without equal.'' He kissed her nose and pushed her away.

They stood and straightened their clothes. It took several moments for his heart to stop racing so he could think clearly.

''What did you bring me?'' He pointed to the laptop on the coffee table.

''A package was delivered to the restaurant with that in it. It's from your boss, Diamond.'' Opening her

purse, she reached in and pulled out the box of disk-
ettes and note. "This accompanied it."

Jon took both. After reading over the note, he set it
aside, opened the laptop and turned it on. The disk-
ettes were numbered. He slipped in the first one. The
directory for the embassy files came up on the opening
screen.

Lauren looked over his shoulder at the laptop screen.
"Are those the files you were working with?"

"Yes, except for this one." He pointed to the one file
labeled Dia.txt. He brought up that one.

Jon,
    I received all your messages. I've accessed the
embassy computer as of 0100 hours your time.
According to my experts here, there have been
several deletions. I'm having my experts try to retrieve the deleted files. Check with me at 1800
hours your time.
    I'll try to pull a security expert from our Dublin
office to check Lauren's apartment. I'll include a
report when you call. Good luck.

Jon ran his fingers through his hair. "I'm not going
to let our mole get away with this. He thinks he's so
damn smart, but he's going to screw up somewhere,
sometime, and I'm going to be there, waiting for him,
ready to take him down."

His obvious anguish touched Lauren, deeper than she
wanted to admit. She rested her hand on his shoulder.
His fingers covered hers and squeezed. He didn't look
up, but Lauren knew he was grateful for her under-
standing and support.

"I need to get back to the restaurant, Jon."

That got his attention. "Why?"

"It seems that everything unraveled the few hours I was gone. I have several messes to sort out when I get back."

He stood and faced her. "How did the police interview go?"

"They have no reason to believe it was anything more than an accident."

Jon's expression hardened. She waited for the argument, but he offered none.

"What about your fiancé and Parker James?"

The man had a memory like her Aunt Milly, who always remembered every little thing you didn't want her to. "I'm impressed you remembered those."

"My life has often depended on whether I remembered details."

It was a reminder she could've done without.

"Parker came by to check on me."

"I don't like that he's that interested in you. It makes me wonder if he has another motive besides friendship."

"I told you before, Parker was a lifesaver after you were declared dead."

"Did anyone else from the embassy offer their support?"

"A couple. But Parker was the most consistent."

Jon stepped closer and picked up the thick braid that hung over her shoulder. He pulled the rubber band from the end and began to unravel the strands.

"I still don't like it. I'll have to keep an extra eye on him."

His fingers in her hair felt heavenly. No, that wasn't the right word. They felt delicious, erotic, carnal. Lauren closed her eyes, wanting to savor the experience.

"You're beautiful," Jon whispered, his lips brushing the skin below her ear. "Do you know what I want to do, sweetheart?"

"No."

"I want to make love to you right here in the middle of the living room, right now."

His declaration snapped her out of her sensuous dream. Her eyes popped open to meet his burning blue gaze. With his eyes the color of Jon's and his face clean shaven, Lauren was inclined to believe all this man's tales. But the nagging fear that everything was not as it should be rose up and seized her heart. Would she ever know the truth—the whole truth without any pieces missing?

Stepping out of his embrace, she murmured, "I have to go." She started for the door.

"Lauren," he called. She paused. "Did you ever contact your fiancé and tell him you can't marry him?"

She swung around to face him. "Don't push me. I'll do what's right for everyone."

"What's that supposed to mean?"

"It means that you can't ride roughshod over my life. If you can't trust me enough to do the right thing, then maybe you'd better slip back into the shadows. You have your files and laptop. I promise I won't give you away."

His hand trailed down her arm. "I'm sorry. I've been going crazy here, thinking about Tony, the mole, wondering what happened to my boss." He laced his fingers through hers. "And you. I've been worried about your safety, concerned you were okay. Missing you." He brought her hand up to his lips. "I'm sorry if I came off like a caveman, but you bring out some primitive feelings in me."

He grinned and a small dimple appeared in his right cheek. Jon had a dimple there.

"Lauren, what is it?" His eyes were tender with concern.

She shook her head. "I have to go."

He released her hand. "I'll be here."

She reached for the doorknob.

"Lauren, be careful going back to the restaurant. Take a couple of cabs, or take the Underground, then a cab."

A pleased grin curved her mouth. "Hey, I already did that coming over here. I might make a decent spy after all."

Lauren bumped into one patron, nearly knocking the man off his feet in her haste to get to the kitchen.

"Jimmy," she called, pushing open the swinging door.

His head jerked up, and he stopped chopping the onion on the cutting board before him. Grabbing his arm, she dragged him into her office, never giving him time to put down his butcher knife.

"What happened while I was gone? Any more disasters?"

Jimmy ran his finger along the top of the knife blade. "The Fazeo brothers showed up with our order, so now we have twice what we need. And then Donald came by."

Lauren's head rolled forward, her loose hair falling around her face. She pushed her hair behind her shoulder, then glanced at Jimmy and saw the question in his eyes as to why her hair was now loose.

"What did Donald say?" Lauren asked, sitting down behind her desk and ignoring Jimmy's silent question.

"He'll call later. How did things go for you?"

"You'll be happy to know our friend answers his door the same way no matter who it is."

Jimmy's fingers flexed around the knife. "Everything okay?"

Holding her head in her hands, she said, "How can I tell?"

He gave her shoulder a gentle squeeze. "It's going to get better. If you need me, you know where to find me."

She smiled at the slender Englishman. "Thanks, you've been a good friend."

"I mean it."

When the door closed behind him, Lauren folded her arms on the desk and rested her head on them. She was lost and didn't have a clue where she was.

Jon pushed away from the table and rubbed his aching temples. Part of the Teltex file stared back at him from the computer screen. He sensed that somehow the mole had accessed the embassy computer and deleted portions of the file. Jon hoped that Diamond's computer doctor would be able to retrieve it.

He wished he had the hard copy of the files so he could compare them to the information on the diskette. It would be the only way he would know *for sure* if the mole had tampered with the information in the existing file.

His stomach growled, reminding him that he hadn't eaten since Lauren had fixed that foul stuff for breakfast.

Lauren. His eyes drifted closed, and he saw her as she appeared last night in his shirt, her long, beautiful legs driving the desire he felt for her into overwhelming passion that had almost exploded beyond his control.

He had to fight the temptation to press her into a physical commitment. She was not ready to give herself to him. But, once he had her safe, he was going to try everything in his power to persuade her that she belonged to him.

He worried about her getting back to her restaurant. She had had enough sense not to come straight to Jimmy's flat from her restaurant. She was right—she would've made a good spy.

But hadn't he inadvertently made her into one by coming to her? Hadn't he plunged her into the netherworld where only the dead and tormented such as himself lived?

His stomach growled again. He was tempted to visit the corner grocer and get some real food, but that would be an unnecessary risk. Sighing, he walked into the kitchen. Sardines and Earl Grey didn't sound too bad.

The afternoon seemed to go on forever. One of Lauren's waiters didn't show, and she filled in when a group of Texans on a tour of London descended on her restaurant. Close to five, Donald called.

"Lauren, where have you been?" he asked, a note of testiness in his voice.

"Things have been crazy around here, Donald."

"You missed our appointment with the jeweler. That is unlike you."

"I'm sorry." She explained about the Ford and added her cover-up story of going to Grasmere.

"Are you all right, sweetheart?"

Oddly enough, the endearment evoked nothing in her. Now, when Jon had called her that . . .

"I'm fine."

"We don't have much time. I'll pick you up at your flat in thirty minutes. Wear your best. I want to impress the Swedish ambassador. There might be some business opportunities for me."

The line was disconnected. Lauren stared stupidly at the handset. Donald had hung up on her. It was unlike him. As she replaced the receiver, it occurred to Lauren what Donald had just said. They were scheduled to attend the Swedish-embassy party tonight.

She couldn't go. Things were crazy enough without this added in. Quickly she redialed Donald's office number. "Is Donald there?" she asked the secretary.

"No. He just departed."

"Rats," she muttered to herself.

"May I take a message, Ms. Michaels?"

"No, thanks. I'll try him at home." It seemed her luck was consistent—all bad.

Glancing at her watch, she decided it was too soon for Donald to be at home, so what choice did she have but to rush home and get ready? Grabbing her purse, she hurried out of her office.

"Jimmy, I've got to go. The Swedish-embassy party. I'll call our friend and let him know where I am."

As she walked home, it occurred to Lauren that going to this party would provide her the perfect opportunity to end things with Donald. And she owed Donald a face-to-face meeting, not a phone call, to break their engagement.

It was obvious to her, after her response to Jon, that her feelings for Donald were more along the line of friendship, not the abiding love or passion that a woman should feel for her mate. It was a startling truth that she had been forced to face over the past few days.

And she had the man calling himself Jonathan Michaels to thank for that.

Thinking of Jon, Lauren knew she had to call him and tell him where she was going. She could let him stew in his own juices, but for what purpose other than vengeance? It wasn't Jon's fault she didn't love Donald enough to marry him. Nor was it Jon's fault that she was attracted to him.

She stopped at a pay phone a block from her flat and dialed Jimmy's number. After the tenth ring, she hung up. Jon, obviously being a good spy, wasn't answering the phone. She needed to work out some code system with him so she could call.

Since she couldn't leave him twisting in the wind all night, her only option was to call the restaurant and talk to Jimmy.

"Jon won't answer your phone. When your shift is over, would you stop by your place and tell Jon what has happened?"

"You're asking a lot, Lauren."

"I know. He's a little abrasive, but—"

"But you know I'll do it."

"That's right. And remind me to give you a raise."

"You can bet on that."

"I knew I could. Oh, and Jimmy?"

"What?"

"Would you take Jon something to eat? Your apartment isn't exactly the culinary highlight of London."

"I'm going to hit you up for a big raise, Lauren."

His brashness amused her. "You'll get it. One other thing, Jimmy. Be careful. Make sure you're not followed."

"Great," he grumbled. "Just what I always wanted to be. A mark in a James Bond movie."

* * *

Parker glanced around the empty warehouse. It made him nervous to come to this place when it was deserted. His footsteps rang out in the quiet as he walked toward the steel stairs tucked in the back corner. If he was trying for an unobtrusive entrance, he failed.

The office door at the head of the steps was open. Parker entered.

"Close the door," the other man ordered. After Parker complied, he asked, "Did you find out where Lauren was last night, and did she say anything about Greg Williams saving her from the car?"

"She claimed a man came out of nowhere to rescue her then disappeared. She acted as if she'd never met him before."

"And do you think she didn't recognize Greg?"

"How could she have not?" Parker shook his head. "I introduced him to Lauren at lunch just the other day. She spent enough time at our table to be able to identify him."

The man behind the desk rubbed his hand over his chin. "So what does that tell us?"

"That she's covering for the man?"

"You're right. But the question is why?"

"How should I know?" Parker snapped.

"Maybe you'd better make it your business to know."

"And how do you suggest I do that?"

"You're the CIA expert. Come up with an idea. And make it quick. We need only one more part. I don't want things fouled up at this stage of the game. Do you understand me?"

Only too clearly, Parker thought. *If he didn't deliver, he'd end up like Anthony Neil—dead.*

* * *

Nervously Jimmy knocked loudly on the door to his flat. Today he had nearly choked on his morning tea when he read the newspaper account of Anthony Neil's murder. He was worried that Lauren trusted this man who was accused of killing his partner. Jimmy didn't share the same confidence in this bloke that his employer did. Why, he hadn't even given Lauren his correct name.

"Who is it?" a voice demanded through the door.

"Jimmy Mason."

The lock sounded, then the door swung open. Jimmy peered into the apartment but didn't see anyone. He didn't like the situation. Growing up on the streets of Liverpool, he learned when to stand and fight and when to cut and run. The latter was demanded now.

He turned, ready to run down the hall, when the same voice growled, "Come in."

He stepped into the room, his back to the wall. The door closed, and he found himself face-to-face with the point of Jon's knife.

"Your habits stink, Yank."

"Where's Lauren? Has something happened to her?"

"She's out with her fiancé."

Jon froze, his knife hovering over its sheath. His eyes turned dark and turbulent.

Uncomfortable with the tense silence, Jimmy quickly explained the situation. "She tried to call you, but you didn't pick up."

Jon assembled his cane with a quick twist.

"Where did they go?"

"The Swedish embassy was having a reception," Jimmy answered. "I think she forgot about the doings until Donald called and reminded her."

"Why didn't she refuse to go?"

"Aside from the fact that Donald is her fiancé?"

Jon's sharp, cold gaze could have cut glass.

"Here." Jimmy shoved the white bag at him. Jon took it, limped to the kitchen table and settled into a chair. Jimmy sat down beside him and watched Jon pull out the aluminum pan filled with chicken *flautas,* quesadillas, rice and fruit tamales.

"You can thank Lauren for the dinner," Jimmy said.

Jon glanced up, the plastic fork included with the dinner clutched in his hand. "You're telling me that you wouldn't have done this on your own?"

Jimmy's eyes narrowed. "Depends."

"On what?"

"On what your intentions are toward Lauren."

"Why are my intentions any of your business?"

"Because I'm Lauren's friend. And I care for her and won't sit by and let someone take advantage of her." It worried Jimmy that Lauren called this man Jon, when the newspapers identified him as Greg Williams.

The man rested his arm on the back of the kitchen chair. "Okay, what do you want to know?"

"I'm curious. Why, of all the people in London, did you turn to Lauren in your time of need? What's she to you?"

Jon took a bite of the *flauta,* thinking of a way to satisfy Jimmy's concern without telling him too much. "She's an old friend. Someone I could trust when the chips were down."

Jimmy crossed his arms over his chest as he studied Jon's face. "I don't recall you ever coming to the restaurant."

"Do you see every customer who eats at Santa Fe Station?"

"No."

"Why, I've even eaten Lauren's blue cornmeal." He hoped the reference to that ghastly stuff would satisfy the Englishman's curiosity. "And lived to tell about it."

Apparently his reference to the cereal worked. Jimmy grimaced. "You're either very brave or very stupid."

He shrugged. "Sometimes with Lauren there isn't a choice."

From his expression Jimmy heartily agreed. He stood. "If you hurt her," he warned the other man, "you'll answer to me.

Jon's eyes were like laser beams, hot, intense, probing. "You love her, don't you?"

Jimmy didn't bother to hide his feelings for Lauren. "Yeah, I love her, but not in the way you mean. She believed in me when no one else did, not even me. She gave me a chance to make somethin' of myself. The last time she was hurt, I couldn't do anything about it. I can now. I don't want to see her go through that pain again."

Jon's spine stiffened. This was his chance to learn firsthand what happened to Lauren three years ago. "What pain?"

"Her husband was killed in a car accident. I've never seen a person grieve so hard. Nearly killed her. That's why I don't want to see you screw up her chances with Donald. He's been good for her. The bleakness that was always in her eyes is gone."

Jon tried to keep his voice neutral. He didn't succeed. "Does she love him?"

"Naw, she doesn't love him, not like she did her first husband. That type of love comes only once in a lifetime. But Lauren likes Donald, and they are compatible. Don't mess things up for her."

Jon watched Jimmy depart. He sat staring at the closed door, hearing again what Jimmy had said. Lauren still loved her husband. He closed his eyes in relief. It would make his job easier.

Chapter 8

Lauren had finished her shower and was wrapped in a towel when the doorbell rang.

"Rats," she murmured, hurrying out of the bathroom. "Who is it?" she called through the closed door.

"Donald." He sounded like a four-year-old who hadn't had his nap.

She opened the door. "I'm running late. Give me ten minutes." Without waiting for his reply, she rushed back into the bedroom.

Yanking out her lingerie drawer, she dug through the bras and panties, searching for the strapless bra she needed to wear with her black sheath. When she spotted it in the back corner, she pulled it out. Along with the bra, something else flew out. Lauren looked down at her feet to see what it was. A pressed white rosebud lay on the floor.

With shaking fingers, she picked it up. This was the rose Jon had given her on their wedding day. They had obtained the marriage license and gone to the local magistrate to get married. On the way inside the building, Jon stopped at a florist and bought her a single white rosebud. He told her it symbolized their love, pure and beginning to bud.

How did the rosebud get in the corner of her lingerie drawer when she had pressed it in her diary? A cold finger of fear stroked down her spine. Where *was* her diary?

She fumbled through the items in the drawer until she came across the red diary near the front: How had it traveled from the back to the front on its own? And how had the rose managed to escape from its pages when the diary had a locking buckle? She had never bothered to lock the book, but she had slid the metal tongue into its groove.

She opened the diary and scanned several pages. The toothbrush incident was recorded, as were her feelings about the first time she and Jon had made love. All things that the man claiming to be her husband had whispered sweetly in her ear.

And hadn't he been waiting for her in her flat the other night? Waiting in this very room?

She took a deep breath, trying to calm herself enough to think. But the magnitude of what she had just discovered rolled over her like a tidal wave, swamping her and drowning her in despair.

The diary and rosebud fell from her nerveless fingers. ''No,'' she moaned, staggering backward and collapsing on the bed. She drew her knees up to her chest, curling into a tight ball.

The intensity of the betrayal flayed her heart. Tears began to seep out from beneath her closed eyes.

Had it all been an elaborate charade to sucker her into believing Jonathan Michaels was still alive? But why? Why would anyone want to pull so cruel a trick on her? What advantage would it be to anyone if she believed Jon alive?

"Lauren, are you ready yet?" Donald impatiently called out.

Donald. His name rang through her brain. So lost had she been in her misery that she'd completely forgotten him, sitting in the other room.

"Not quite," she answered, struggling to sit up. "Give me a few more moments."

"Lauren, it is very important I be on time." Now, instead of a sulky boy, he sounded like a father reprimanding an errant child. "I have to meet this Polish businessman who is wanting our firm to service several of his operations."

Good old Donald. Business before anything else, even his heart. Or maybe his work was the true love of his life and she was simply an afterthought.

"If I'm not ready in five minutes," she called out, anger quickly replacing the raw pain, "leave without me."

"Really, Lauren," came his indignant reply.

Wiping the tears from her face, she stood. She saw the diary and the rosebud lying on the floor. Picking them up, she paused, then brought the rosebud up to her nose. The sweet smell of the flower remained trapped within the dried, pressed petals. That day had been so special, one of the happiest days of her life. She shook off the memory. She felt like that rose, drained of all life and a shell of herself. Placing the rose inside her diary, she returned them to the drawer.

With a steely determination, she promised herself she'd make it through this night, just as she had the countless other times when the pain in her heart had been achingly intense.

As for Donald and the Jon impostor, they would get what they deserved.

Nine minutes and thirty-four seconds later, she stepped out of the bedroom, dressed in a black chiffon sheath with spaghetti straps. Her hair was twisted into a French roll, a pearl comb holding her style in place. Rhinestone earrings were the only jewelry she wore. Her evening jacket was folded over her arm.

Donald surveyed her from head to toe and nodded his approval. He helped her on with her jacket, then brushed a sexless kiss across her cheek. "We need to hurry." He headed for the door, expecting her to follow like a well-trained dog.

Irritation spurted through her veins. She had nearly killed herself to get ready, and all he could do was nod?

She'd had enough of men at the moment and wished they all would vanish off the planet.

Pausing at the door, he glanced over his shoulder. "Are you coming?"

He was definitely peeved with her, but it was filtered through his proper British upbringing. Well, too bad.

"Yes." *And you'll probably wish I hadn't.*

Donald's dark green Jaguar was parked in front of her building. He opened the passenger door and waited patiently for her to be seated.

"Buckle your seat belt," he commanded as he shut the door.

As they drove through the city to the embassy, Lauren acknowledged to herself that Donald didn't deserve the lion's share of her anger. She had been well aware of his passion for business when she agreed to marry him, so she deserved part of the blame.

"Lauren, why haven't you mailed the invitations for your bridal shower? I saw them on the table. Weren't they supposed to be posted by Wednesday at the latest?"

Her life was crashing down around her ears, and Donald was worried about invitations. "I forgot."

"You know, you've been acting strangely lately." Donald's voice seemed excessively loud in the small confines of the car. "Why, even Father has commented on your odd behavior."

"It's just stress, Donald. I've got a lot on my mind."

"But how could you have forgotten our appointment with the jeweler?" he asked as he pulled into the driveway of the Swedish embassy.

Believe me, it wasn't hard. The thought popped into her head. Lauren glanced at him. He deserved an explanation, if not an apology. "I'm sorry, Donald. I'll admit it was rude of me not to call. But it simply slipped my mind. The accident did shake me up."

"Accident?" He frowned, then said, "Ah, yes, the one your cook told me about." He pulled up to the front door, got out, motioning for her to do the same in order to allow the attendant to park the car. "Well, I hope this tendency of yours disappears quickly," he muttered as he took her arm to walk her to the door.

Lauren stared at him in disbelief. He wasn't concerned for her safety or glad she wasn't hurt. No, he was simply annoyed she'd missed their appointment. That did it.

"Donald, we need to talk."

Unaware of her reaction, he continued moving her into the building. "In a moment, dear. I have to see if Mr. Kowalski is here." He dashed through the crowd, leaving her by the front door.

The temptation to turn around and walk out was enticing for Lauren. But that would be cowardly, she told herself. It would also put off her confrontation with Donald. And she wanted that over as soon as possible.

A waiter strode by with a tray of drinks. Lauren grabbed a glass of champagne.

"What's the matter with you?" Donald asked, suddenly reappearing, taking the drink from her hand. "You know alcohol makes you sick. I don't need you disgracing yourself in front of Mr. Kowalski like you did with Mr. Reins." He spoke to the waiter. "Do you have any ginger ale?"

"At the bar."

Donald placed his hand on her back and steered her through the crowd to the corner bar. The feel of his hand on her bare skin made her muscles stiffen. Never before had Donald's touch made her want to draw away from him. It was an intimacy she should've welcomed. She didn't.

Apparently her reaction got his attention. "What is wrong with you?"

"Donald, I need to talk to you."

"Not now, Lauren. After you meet Mr. Kowalski, we'll have time to talk."

"No, now."

"Lauren," he urged, taking a step closer to her. "That's Kowalski coming toward us. Smile."

Lauren tried to make polite small talk with the handsome young man through her brittle smile. But each time Donald put a hand on her, her shoulder, her back, her waist, she stepped away from his touch. She tried not to make it obvious, but finally Kowalski commented.

"Is something wrong, Ms. Michaels?"

Lauren felt Donald go stiff and out of the corner of her eye she saw his cheeks turn an unbecoming shade of red.

"No, of course not. Donald is a wonderful businessman. You'll be very satisfied with his company."

They chatted courteously for a few more minutes before Kowalski excused himself. Donald grasped her arm and led her out the French doors onto the balcony.

"I've never been so embarrassed in my entire life as I just was a moment ago in front of that man. Would you care to explain your behavior?" Donald demanded. His eyes bulged with his anger. "You could've cost me Kowalski's business."

His response floored her. "Is that all you can think about, Donald? Your business?"

"What would you have me think about?" he countered. From his expression he probably didn't have a clue as to why she was upset.

"I've been trying to tell you something since the moment we stepped into the embassy, only you've refused to listen."

"Well, I'll say your timing is most inappropriate, Lauren. Why couldn't it have waited until we went back to your flat?"

She had tried to wait, but he had kept touching her and her body had reacted without consulting her brain. "Donald, I can't marry you."

His expression didn't change. "Quit kidding. Now, tell me what is troubling you."

"You don't believe me?"

"Of course not. Why would you want to end our engagement?"

"How about the fact that you don't love me as much as you love your precious catering business? I come in a poor second to canapés." Her voice rose with each word.

He glanced around to make sure they had not attracted a crowd. "Lauren, please, lower your voice."

"That's a perfect example. You're more worried about creating a scene than about the fact I just told you I don't want to marry you."

"You're being ridiculous."

"Am I?"

"Of course."

"Well, then let me make it perfectly clear. You don't love me. But that's okay, because I don't love you…not the way I should." She couldn't meet his eyes at that moment, not after what she'd just said. She tried to push past him, but he caught her arm.

"Lauren," he chided, "you're being too emotional about this."

She glanced down at his hand on her upper arm, then at his face. "Let go of me, Donald, or I'll not be responsible for what I do."

The threat in her voice got through to him. He abruptly released her and stepped away. It was then that Lauren noticed they had drawn a crowd. With her head held high, she marched through the onlookers.

She called a cab and waited for it outside the embassy gate. She hadn't meant for the gathered throng to hear her break her engagement, but they had. Donald was probably more upset by the fact others had heard than by the fact that she'd ended their relationship.

She glanced up into the clear evening sky. It had been a jim-dandy day. If the sky fell down on her, it wouldn't surprise her.

The taxi honked. Shaking off her depressing thoughts, she climbed into the back seat.

"Where to?" the cabbie asked.

She should go back to Jimmy's flat and confront her impostor with her diary. But she was too tired for that right now. She wanted to go back to her own little flat, crawl under the covers and go to sleep. Tomorrow would be soon enough to cross swords with the man who claimed to be Jon.

She gave the cabbie the address of her flat.

Jon paced around the small confines of the living room. He had given up trying to concentrate on the computer files a half hour ago. Jealousy and worry had eaten at him like battery acid, burning away every other thought but Lauren.

He paused and glanced at his watch for the tenth time in the past five minutes—1700 hours. Lauren had been gone four hours and thirty-seven minutes.

He was tempted to go over to the Swedish embassy and pluck Lauren out of Donald Blake's clutches. Then he would take her back to her apartment and make love to her until her mind was so full of him that there was no room for any other man.

"You're thinking like a trained idiot," he muttered sarcastically to himself. What use was he to anyone when all he could think about was Lauren? Was she safe? Was she enjoying herself with Donald?

The thoughts were driving him crazy. Since he wasn't making any progress here, he might as well go to Lauren's flat and wait for her fiancé to bring her home. He would check out the flat and make sure it was safe, he told himself.

Before he left, he decided to call his boss. Maybe this time Diamond would be there.

Luck was with him, because Diamond picked up after the first ring. "Hello."

"Diamond, this is Sapphire."

"I'm glad you called. Did you get my package?"

"Yeah, it's been delivered. What's been going on? I've tried for two days to contact you."

"All hell has broken loose. You want to know about the disaster in the Middle East? Or how about the singleton I had to pull in Beijing? Or about the Central African—"

"I get the idea."

"Give me your number."

Until now Jon hadn't felt safe leaving his number and location on a recorder. Anyone with access to Diamond's office could have gotten the information, and enough had already gone wrong in this investigation. He didn't need any more problems. He rattled off the number. "Were you able to get someone to check out Lauren's apartment?"

"You lucked out, partner. You remember Carol Holland?"

He remembered Carol from the time they were stationed together in Poland. "Yeah."

"Well, she was en route to Washington from her latest posting. She was at Gatwick so she checked out Lauren's place. It was free of any bugs, and Carol didn't see any signs that the place was being watched. But she did report she ran into a woman coming out of Lauren's apartment. After Carol described the woman, we discovered it was Lauren herself. That wasn't smart of you to let her go there before it was checked out.''

"I didn't have a choice. I told her not to go. She didn't listen.''

There was a long silence at the other end. Finally Diamond asked, "How hard did you try?"

The question slammed into Jon with the force of a high-speed train. Had he tried hard enough to stop Lauren? Or had he on some deep, unconscious level let her go out as bait? It was a sickening thought. "You must think I'm a sorry SOB if you think I didn't try to stop her.''

"Vengeance is a powerful motivation.''

"Vengeance against who? Lauren? You're out of your ever-loving mind if you think that.''

"Against the mole.''

"And you think I would put Lauren in an unsafe position just so I could use her as bait.''

There was a long pause. "No, but I had to ask.''

"Yeah, but I don't have to like it one damn bit.''

"Sapphire. Sapphire?''

"What?''

"There's been another theft from a NATO contractor.''

That information snapped him out of his dark thoughts. "Who?''

"Jensen Brothers, headquartered in Amsterdam. This theft didn't occur on sight. It happened when the part was shipped to its final destination to be put together with—''

"The other components that were missing?''

"Bingo.''

"Tony and I wondered if those parts went together, but the people in the companies didn't know.''

"That's because they weren't told. I've got a friend in naval intelligence. We went to lunch today. While he was in my office, he saw the name of the company in Amsterdam and asked me about it. After we did some dancing around, he fessed up that that manufacturer was working on a new radar system for NATO."

Jon grinned at the thought of Diamond trying to pump his friend for information and vice versa. It must have been quite a sight.

"The program was designed by a man named Alfred Fox. After the numerous thefts of NATO technology, the program director decided to break up the new radar system into key components and parcel them out to different manufacturers. None of the manufacturers knew of the others and none knew what they were making."

"No wonder we had so much trouble."

"Apparently our mole obtained the plans and started systematically stealing the individual parts. With this last theft, he now owns one complete system."

Jon cursed, a crude Anglo-Saxon profanity.

"My sentiments exactly. Now the only question is, to whom is our mole going to market the system?"

The feeling of helplessness that had settled over Jon while he was in the hospital rested again on his shoulders.

"How long ago did the burglary occur?"

"A couple of days."

"How did you find out about it?"

"It was reported to NATO officials."

"There's a common thread that ties all these thefts together—I know it, Diamond. Tony found it and died because he knew. And when I discover what it is, I think we'll be able to pinpoint who is working with our mole and how their ROSES network operates." Tony had originally come up with the moniker for the spy ring using the first letter of the name of each of the first five companies that had had secrets stolen. The acronym had stuck. "Who at London station knew about the radar system?"

"I don't know. Since naval intelligence was the one guarding the plans, I'll have to contact my friend."

"So while we are losing agents and trying to figure out what's going down, the brains in the Office of Naval Intelligence are sitting on their butts, guarding their information."

"You know how this game is played."

"Yeah, and it sucks."

"When humans change their basic nature, then things will change."

Jon knew exactly what Diamond was talking about. Count on the worst from a person, because you usually got it. "Can you get me Alfred Fox's address and number? Maybe the mole stole the plans at their source."

"All right. And I'll check and see who in London had access to the radar plans."

"I'll keep looking through the files I have to see if I can find the common link. Also, can you find out for me how that last robbery took place?"

"Sure. Take care."

Jon hung up the phone and leaned back against the sofa. It was a radar system that was the cause of the latest thefts. Had Tony known that or had he simply discovered how the prototypes were stolen so easily from each of these high-security plants?

Why hadn't the ONI come clean with them and told them how the thefts had been connected? They might have been able to prevent this last one. Too bad all the intelligence agencies in the U.S. government didn't realize they were all working for the same goal.

Jon's knuckles gripped the head of his cane with such force that the metal cut into his skin. He wrestled with his anger against the petty men who had to have their little empires at the cost of Tony's life.

He stood, fighting the building rage. Suddenly it erupted, and he smashed the lamp on the end table with his cane. Why did Tony have to be sacrificed?

What about Lauren? a voice in his head asked. Would she end up like Tony, the victim of the spy game he played? Was he any different from the men responsible for Tony's death? Hadn't he inadvertently contaminated Lauren by contacting her?

He didn't have an answer. But he knew that he couldn't sit here another moment. He was going to her flat to wait for her. And if she wasn't home by midnight, he was going to the Swedish embassy, no matter what.

When Lauren climbed out of the cab in front of her building, Donald was waiting for her.

Lauren paid the cabbie and turned to Donald. They might as well finish what they had started at the embassy. She was surprised that Donald had taken time out of his business negotiations to come after her.

"I want to talk to you, Lauren."

She leaned against his Jaguar. "Go ahead."

"Can we go inside?"

"No. Whatever you have to say to me can be said out here."

"What has gotten into you lately? You are behaving most irrationally. Nothing like your normal self."

"You're wrong, Donald. I've finally found the rest of me." She laid her hand on his arm. The man deserved an explanation. "You're a good man. And our time together has been quiet and pleasant. It was easy for us. But I am not the love of your life, Donald. And that's what I want to be."

"You are being silly. Marriages based on friendship work much better than those of burning passion."

"Maybe for you. Not for me." She leaned up and kissed his cheek. "I'm sorry. Goodbye."

He looked as if he wanted to argue. Instead, he got in his car and drove off.

"That might have been the stupidest thing you've ever done," she told herself. "Toss away the good one and keep the iffy one." Of course, if she had her way, she would toss the iffy one, too.

Exhaustion weighed heavily on her as she walked down the hall to her flat. She shrugged out of her jacket, then dragged her keys from her purse and unlocked the door. She didn't bother to turn on the hall light but stepped inside. Suddenly the door closed behind her, and one large hand clamped over her mouth, while other slid around her waist. Her attacker hauled her tight against his chest. Jacket, purse and keys spilled to the floor.

Lauren began to struggle against the confining hold.

"Stop it, Lauren. It's Jon." The words were hissed in her ear.

It was the final blow to her already bruised heart. She abruptly stopped her struggle. Jon waited a few seconds, then released her. The knowledge that it was "Impostor Jon" who had grabbed her exploded like a bomb in Lauren's brain, and all she could see was red. Suddenly she screamed. A heartfelt shriek of frustration and pain. Jon clamped his hand over her mouth and hauled her against him.

"Dammit, Lauren, what's wrong with you?" He dragged her to him, their bodies touching shoulder to hip. Slowly he removed his hand from her mouth.

"Let me go, you bastard."

His eyes narrowed. "What happened?"

She struggled against him, but his hand cupped her chin and forced her gaze to his. "You're not going anywhere until you tell me what's happened."

"I found out about you, you low-down, sneaky, two-faced impostor."

"What is that supposed to mean?"

Before she could answer him, there was a furious pounding on her front door.

"Lauren, honey, you all right?"

She immediately recognized Cassie's voice. "Let me go," she whispered to Jon. He hesitated.

"Lauren, is anything wrong?" Cassie yelled.

"You'd better let me go, or Cassie will call the cops for sure."

He released his hold on her, and Lauren scrambled away from him. Jon reached for his cane, then hobbled into the living room. When he was out of sight, Lauren limped to the door, one heel off, one on, because of their struggle, and opened it.

"Hi, Cass." She tried to sound casual, but her hair was falling out of the French twist, and one of the straps of her dress had slipped off her shoulder.

"Are you all right, luv? I heard this awful scream coming from your flat and was worried about you." Cassie peered around Lauren into the empty hall. "Anything wrong that I should know about?" she whispered in a conspiratorial tone.

Lauren glanced over her shoulder and saw her jacket, purse and keys lying on the floor. Cassie was going to need a good story to explain Lauren's condition and the noise that had come from her flat. *Stick as close to the truth as you can,* a voice inside her head advised.

"I don't know if you saw Donald and me out by the curb a few minutes ago, but I ended our engagement tonight. Donald was more concerned about creating a scene in public than anything else."

Cassie shook her head. "I'm sorry, luv. Men can be such pigs."

The comment, spoken with such wonderful British elegance, brought a smile to Lauren's face. "I agree. Unfortunately I was rather upset when I got into my flat...and I guess I threw a tantrum. One of those 'scream bloody murder and throw yourself on the floor' kind of things." She leaned forward. "It's rather embarrassing."

Cassie patted her arm. "It's understandable. Are you okay? You didn't hurt anything?"

"I'm fine. Really."

"If you need a shoulder to cry on or someone to trade misery with, you know where to find me."

"Thanks, Cassie. You're a good friend."

Lauren closed the door and leaned back against it. She had just lied with an ease that disturbed her. It was a habit that she'd managed to pick up since the man in the other room had appeared in her life.

Taking a deep, fortifying breath, Lauren pushed away from the door. There were some salient points that needed to be addressed by that man. And she was going to get some truthful answers out of him if it killed her.

Chapter 9

Lauren found him in the living room, sitting on the couch, his cane in his hands. When she entered the room, he didn't move. Kicking off her remaining shoe, she turned on a lamp. She wanted to see this man's eyes when she confronted him with the truth.

"You broke your engagement to Donald tonight?" he quietly asked.

"You hear well."

He shrugged but offered no comment.

The edge of her rage had been blunted somewhat, but it was still there. She began to pace.

He sighed and the sound brought to mind the picture of a man weary with life. "All right, Lauren, tell me why you're angry with me."

She froze and stared at him. "You lied to me."

His hand massaged the back of his neck. "What specifically are you talking about?"

"You mean that you've lied to me so many times that I need to pinpoint which one I'm furious about?"

"What do you want me to say, Lauren?"

"Oh, I don't know." She gestured wildly with her hand. "Maybe that you're sorry for lying to me. Of course, if you hadn't been caught, you probably wouldn't be trying to worm your way out of the situation now. But I do have a little bit of advice for you." She leaned toward him. "Next time you go through a woman's diary, you should be more careful. Check to make sure you don't drop anything out of it. But I thought they taught you spies better than that."

"Oh."

Her mouth fell open in surprise. "'Oh'? Is that all you have to say? 'Oh.'" She could feel her emotions slipping out of control.

His fingers played over the head of his cane. "It wouldn't do me any good to deny it, would it?"

She couldn't believe her ears. He was calmly sitting there admitting he had read her diary. "Not a bit."

"Well, then what is your point?"

The temptation to grab the lamp off the end table and smash it over his head was overwhelming. But if she gave in to the primitive emotion and knocked him out, she wouldn't get any satisfactory answers from him.

"I want you to tell me who you really are." Her voice quivered with rage. "And why you're masquerading as Jonathan."

"What fell out of the diary?" he asked.

Lauren gritted her teeth. So he wasn't going to answer her question. "What does that have to do with anything? You're caught, buddy, red-handed. And if you have the sense of a goose, you'll tell me who you are."

"What fell out?" It was his tone, soft and steely, that told Lauren if she wanted any response from him, she would have to answer his question.

"A rosebud."

He closed his eyes and rested his head against the cushions. "White. On our way in to see the magistrate to get married, there was a little florist shop next door. I raced in and bought it for you." He looked at her. "Go check in your diary. That isn't recorded. Yes, I thumbed through it. I wanted to see what your thoughts were."

She ran into her bedroom and snatched the diary from the drawer. She switched on the lamp on the nightstand and opened the book. After glancing through the first few pages, which started on their wedding day, she knew the incident hadn't been recorded.

When she glanced up, he was standing in the doorway. "Believe me?"

His answer fit too neatly. And each time she believed him, something turned up to make her doubt. "No."

He limped over to the bed, leaning heavily on his cane, and sat. Lauren jumped to her feet. She didn't want to be near him.

"Ask me something else."

She glared at him.

"Do you want me to tell you about the first time we made love? It was in your office. I'd come back from a trip and raced straight to your restaurant. It was the middle of the afternoon, We locked the door and made love on the desk. After that afternoon, we decided to get married."

The sinking sensation in her stomach told her she was losing this battle. "How do I know you're not lying again?"

"Don't you remember? You had on purple panties and a matching bra."

He hit the nail on the head. "You might have overheard Jon mention it."

"Lauren, do you think I would betray you in that way?"

A sob caught in her throat. "Betray? Oh, you're a fine one to talk to me about betrayal." Her voice shook. "If Jon was a spy and he was caught, maybe he was brainwashed and told you all his secrets." She was grasping at straws and she knew it. "Maybe he was put in a cell with you, and he was hurt and out of his mind and said those things."

"Now who's the one with the wild imagination? You should've been a spy."

"Stop it." She wanted to shout it, but she remembered Cassie across the hall.

"No matter how many questions you ask me and I answer correctly, you'll come up with an excuse as to why I know the answer."

Each word out of his mouth, he was tearing down her defenses. He had a logical explanation for every one of her arguments. "There are too many pieces to the puzzle that don't fit right," she protested.

He stood and moved toward her. She retreated until her back was against the wall. He reached out and lightly ran his fingers along her chin. "Lauren, *lieveling,* trust your heart."

The heart he asked her to trust contracted with pain. And longing. *Lieveling.* Jon had called her that only when his guard was down and his passion was ruling him. It hurt to hear the Dutch endearment falling from this man's lips.

Before she could react in any way, his mouth covered hers. It was a soft, gentling kiss. He didn't overwhelm her or use the strength of the passion she felt lying beneath his steely surface. Instead, he seduced with a light touch, his lips skimming over hers, teasing.

He trailed kisses across her cheek to her ear. "Do you remember the first time I called you *lieveling?*" He pulled back to look into her eyes.

This time the shock of hearing him call her that wasn't as great as it had been when he first uttered it. "Yes."

"We were making love for the first time, and I whispered it in your ear. You went still and asked me what it meant. My mind was clouded with, uh, need, and you wanted an explanation." His smile was self-mocking. "It nearly killed me to answer you."

Lauren had the most absurd urge to giggle. She remembered his dazed expression when she'd asked that question. It had taken him several moments to answer.

He pulled the pearl comb and bobby pins from her hair, then ran his fingers through the waist-length strands. "I told you it was Dutch for *darling,*" he absently added, his attention focused on her hair. The feel of his strong hands on her head was distracting.

You can't afford to give in to your feelings, her conscience warned. *What lie is he telling you now?* "Your father was Dutch," she said. It seemed her mouth was working independently of her brain.

A smile of pure pleasure curved his lips. "It was my mother, and you know it."

"I never forgot anything about Jon." She meant to drive him off with her response.

His hands cradled her face. "Your soul knows mine, Lauren. Let me love you."

The hypnotic power of his blue eyes was pulling her to him, breaking the bonds of restraint she tried to impose. She closed her eyes, hoping against hope to counteract his pull.

He kissed the sensitive spot on the underside of her jaw. Closed in to a world of only sensation, Lauren's body responded to him, ignoring the dictates of her mind. It felt right to be held by this man, as if she had come home after a long, tiring journey. His hands ran over her shoulders, then down her back. Gently he pressed her into his body.

This was Jonathan Michaels, her husband, her mind yelled. With that final thought, her brain shut down and her senses took control. She slid her arms around his neck and settled her mouth on his. He instantly responded by sliding his tongue into her mouth. The taste and rhythm was familiar, the joy known but too long denied.

He broke off the kiss, his chest heaving with the exertion of breathing. "I'd sweep you up in my arms and carry you to bed, but we'd both end up on the floor, and besides, we're already here."

She smiled at him. "I've spent more time on the floor with you than I care to think about."

His fingers skimmed along her shoulders and down her arms. "Turn around and I'll unzip you."

Suddenly she was scared. He paused and gave her a reassuring smile. It was unnerving how well he read her, but then again Jon had always known what was going on in her head. If she didn't know better, she'd swear he was a mind reader.

Or a man she'd made love to countless times.

"Do you want me to go first?" he asked, pulling his shirt out of his pants and quickly unbuttoning it. Lauren clearly remembered the sight of his chest. He was well-muscled and lean. He must have worked with weights while he was recovering.

He sat on the bed and took off his shoes and socks.

Standing, he unzipped his pants and cast them aside.

"I'm not a very pretty sight to look at," he said, glancing down at his legs.

She sensed his uncertainty that she might find his scars repulsive. "Turn around," she softly commanded. His brow arched, but he said nothing. He turned his back to her.

He had half a dozen scars on his back. Some were small, but some were several inches in length. There were two that looked as if he'd had major surgery. Her fingers traced the smaller ones. Tears welled in her eyes. How he must've suffered.

"What are you doing?" he asked.

"Shh." Her fingers skimmed over the largest scar, then she bent forward and kissed it. She repeated the action with all the other scars. Finally she slipped her arms around his waist and rested her head against his back.

His hands covered hers, and he squeezed hard. Lauren felt how his chest heaved with each breath. He threw his head back and drew in a deep breath of air. "Ah, *lieveling,* what you do to me." His hand moved hers down to cover his arousal. "I am not the man of steel."

She couldn't resist the temptation. "You certainly could've fooled me."

With a low growl he turned. "You'll pay for that."

"Oh, yeah, how?"

He pushed back the hair that had fallen in her face. All the humor had left his face, and his eyes turned dark with passion. "Lauren, I need you."

And she needed him. "Help me with my zipper," she said, presenting her back to him.

He unzipped her dress and spread the sides wide, then quickly unhooked her bra. His large warm hands skimmed down her back. He placed several kisses along her spine. With agonizing slowness he slid his fingers under the one remaining spaghetti strap of her dress and eased it down her arm. The dress and the bra pooled at her feet, leaving her clothed in her panties, garter belt and hose.

He drew her back against his chest, and his hands covered her breasts. A dart of pleasure pierced her heart, making Lauren's knees weak. Her head rolled back against his shoulder.

"You were always sensitive here," he whispered, stroking her breasts.

The pleasure grew intense, and she turned in his arms. Their mouths met with the savage hunger that had been building in both of them.

He backed toward the bed, his hands working to unhook her garter belt. Lauren joined him in his efforts and they quickly stripped each other of their remaining clothes and lay across the bed.

His eyes, then his hands, traveled over her form, working a familiar magic on her body, taking her to that special place where there was only color and feeling, leaving behind the everyday world with all its worries and cares.

His head bent and he captured her right breast with his lips. The walls of her life seemed to fall in on themselves, consumed by the fire he was building in her. The heat and flames ate up any remaining reservations she had about making love with him.

He lifted his head. "Your body knows me, Lauren. It responds to me as sweetly now as it did three years ago. Do you feel it?" His hands covered her breasts. "You see how your body tells mine of its need?" He didn't wait for her to respond. Instead, he settled his hips over hers. After making sure she was ready for him, he entered her with one smooth thrust.

He stilled, resting his forehead on hers. "I'm home," he murmured in her ear. His hands cradled her face, and his eyes locked with hers. "This is what kept me going. This bond, *lieveling*. Your soul joined to mine. You were the light in my darkness."

A tear escaped the corner of her eye. She reached up and touched the scar on his cheek. He closed his eyes, and his body began to tremble.

"Put your legs around my waist," he gasped, and began to thrust into her. "I want you with me when I reach the top of the mountain."

Lauren felt as if she was caught up in a whirlwind, carried along with this man's intense passion. Suddenly the world exploded in color and light, and then she heard his hoarse shout of completion.

He rested his head in the hollow between her neck and shoulder and lightly kissed the tender skin there. And it was at that exact moment that all doubts about him vanished. Every time she and Jon had made love, he had always kissed her neck in that exact spot.

When she opened her eyes, she met Jon's intense blue gaze. "Do you know now? What does your heart tell you?"

"Yes. I know. You're Jonathan Edward Michaels. My husband."

* * *

Something deep inside Jon eased with her answer. She believed him. He didn't know what he would've done if she hadn't. This had been his last chance.

He rolled off her and gathered her into his arms. She snuggled against him. Her finger traced the outline of one scar that ran from his back, around his side, ending just above his hipbone.

"You keep that up and I'll be ready for a second go around."

She kissed his neck. "As I recall, it doesn't take much with you."

He liked the sound of her laugh. It was untouched by lies and double crosses. It was the sound of someone who was at peace with herself. It was a sound that never passed his lips. Not in recent years.

He tipped up her chin. "I don't want to be greedy our first time together in so long."

He felt the sensuous smile that curved her lips all the way to his toes. "Be greedy."

He was not a man to ignore a woman's invitation. This time he didn't try to rein in the driving hunger he felt for Lauren. Before, he had feared scaring her with his fierceness and intensity. She had been skittish and doubtful, and he knew brute power would have only pushed her away. His entire future had rested on her believing in him, and it had nearly killed him to hold back.

He pulled Lauren on top of him. Surprise showed on her face.

"My knee isn't going to stand up to a second round."

"Are you sure the rest of you will hold up better?"

"Just wait and see."

As he framed her face with his hands, his mouth devoured hers. Her dark hair fell around them, closing them in their own little world.

He couldn't seem to get enough of her. They had just made love minutes before, yet here he was with the stamina of a sixteen-year-old, ready to go again.

Lauren seemed to welcome his intensity. Her fragrance was made up of roses and woman, a lethal combination.

Grasping her hips, he settled her on him. The feel of her taking him into her body, surrounding him with her heat, was glorious and golden. He began to thrust up, and she met his aggressiveness with her own. When they crashed through the clouds together, Jon's heart felt peace for the second time in three years.

Jon woke to the feel of Lauren in his arms. He savored the softness of her body pressed against his. He wondered if he was in some fevered dream and if, when he woke, Lauren would still be there.

"What time is it?" she mumbled, her lips tickling his neck.

He glanced at the wristwatch. "It's a little past three."

She made a contented sound as she snuggled deeper against him.

Now that his body was rested and relaxed, his mind turned again to the concern that had brought him to Lauren's apartment. "Lauren, what happened with Donald tonight? Why did you arrive here in a taxi?"

Absently her fingers toyed with the hair on his chest. The action brought his body to life. His hand covered hers, stilling the movement.

"I'm sure you heard me tell Cassie I broke my engagement to Donald."

She was leaving out a large chunk of the story, and he knew it. "Yes, but there's more to it, isn't there?"

A wry smile curved her lips. "He was irritated that I humiliated him at the embassy party."

"And how did you do that?"

"Other people overheard when I told him that he loved his canapés more than he did me." She shrugged. "The truth didn't faze him. He was more upset over our public spat than he was with me breaking the engagement."

His fingers caught her chin and brought her gaze to his. "The man is a fool. You deserve better than that." His words weren't only directed at the hapless Donald. They were directed at himself, as well.

"You're right. I do." Silently she studied him, then rose up on her elbow. "Tell me, what are you doing here? I thought you needed to lay low."

He hesitated, then said, "I was worried about you."

"Worried?" There was a penetrating look in her eyes. "Is that all it was?"

He brushed her hair back from her face. "I broke the rules again for you. I shouldn't have been wandering around the streets of London, but I discovered I didn't like the idea of you being out with Donald."

Her face lit with pleasure. "You were jealous."

It was a statement, not a question—one that didn't need an answer. She rested her head on his shoulder.

"I talked with my boss tonight."

"Oh? What did he say?"

"He asked me why I allowed you to come to your apartment before it was checked out."

A deep flush stained her cheeks.

"Would you like to know why he said that?"

She sat up and wrapped her arms around her knees. "No, but I'm sure you're going to tell me."

"You're darn right I'm going to tell you." He sat up and faced her. "Me risking my life for this job is one thing. I knew the dangers when I signed my name on the dotted line. But you—there's no reason for you to put yourself at risk."

"Jon, we've had this conversation."

"And we're going to have it again until you understand that this game that's being played out is for real and the stakes are life and death."

"The place was empty. Nothing happened."

"Dumb luck. You could've easily run into someone here, looking through your things, wondering if you knew where I was. You nearly flattened our agent when she came into the building."

A puzzled frown knitted her brows. "That old lady?"

"Maybe she wasn't an old lady. Maybe it was a disguise." His hand settled on the back of her head. "In the world I live in, and in which you are now living, nothing is as it seems. Trust is not a commodity we traffic in. Deceit is. Trust no one."

She jerked her head out of his grasp. "Does that include you?"

"Sh—" He rolled away and sat on the side of the bed, his back to her. He cursed himself for being such a fool. In his attempt to impress upon her the necessity of being careful, he'd undercut his own cause.

Maybe it was time to test the bond they'd just forged. Turning back to her he asked, "Do you think I meant myself?"

Her eyes searched his, and he remained still while she struggled with herself. "No, you didn't mean yourself."

Cupping her cheek, he asked, "Do you trust me?"

Her gaze fell to the blankets.

Everything depended on her trusting him. "Lauren."

"I trust you with my safety." She looked at him. "I know you'd guard me with your life."

There was a hell of a lot that she hadn't said. A big, gaping hole in her trust that he could drive a tank through. "What is it you won't trust me with?"

She looked away, then finally, after taking a deep breath, she met his gaze. "My heart. I don't know if I can ever trust you with that again."

Jon jerked backward with the force of the emotional blow she'd just delivered. He stood and pulled on his briefs. Why didn't she pick up his cane, unlock the stiletto and run it through his heart? The effect would be the same.

He glanced back at the bed. She was studying him, her face lined with worry. "It doesn't pay to be too inquisitive sometimes, does it?"

She shook her head.

Damn. Damn. Damn. The price he paid every year to live in the shadows was becoming greater and greater. And he didn't know if he could pay it anymore.

"Go back to sleep, Lauren."

He walked to the door.

"Where are you going?"

"I'm going to try to figure out what our next move is."

He stretched out on the couch. If she thought he was going to quit and go away, she was dead wrong. He was fighting for their future.

Lauren sat trembling on the bed. This night had been a mad roller-coaster ride. First she discovered Jon had read her diary, and she was sure she'd caught a fake. That was followed by her dazzling evening with Donald and the realization of how little she really meant to him. Finally she'd come home to discover Jon lying in wait, followed by the wringing confrontation, ending up in the earth-shattering session of lovemaking.

Lauren stretched out, and her fingers skimmed over the indentation his head had made on the other pillow. Jon. Her husband. It was a dream come true. But now that she was awake, hurts and doubts were springing up in her heart.

When he'd asked her if she trusted him, she'd started to answer immediately, but something had stopped her. She had no doubt the man in the other room would risk his life to save hers. And she would without hesitation trust him with her safety.

But her heart? Ah, that was a different question. At this point it was impossible for her to give him that. Maybe at some point in the future she could. But not now. The last time he'd had it, he'd thrown it away.

The pounding on the front door woke Lauren. Her eyes flew open and she sat up. Jon shoved her silk kimono robe at her.

"Here, put this on and answer the door." He was still dressed only in his briefs. She tried not to stare.

"Do you know who it is?" she asked.

"No."

While she slipped into her robe, Jon pulled on his pants.

"Lauren," called the man at the door.

She froze and glanced at Jon. "Parker."

"Hurry and answer it."

Out of the corner of her eye, she saw Jon reach for his cane. "Just a minute," she yelled, hurrying toward the front door. She unhooked the security chain and twisted the dead bolt.

"Hello, Parker." Her fingers held together the top edges of her blue kimono.

His eyes traveled from her disheveled hair to her bare feet. "Did I wake you?"

She gave him a half smile. "Yes."

He glanced at his wristwatch. "It's almost ten."

She didn't feel a need to excuse her action but simply remained quiet.

"I'm sorry, Lauren." He wore the proper expression of contrition. "It's just that I was worried about you, hoping that you didn't do anything foolish."

"Why were you worried about me?"

"You haven't seen the paper this morning, have you?"

It was a good assumption since he'd dragged her from bed. But she was well mannered enough not to point that out. "No, I haven't."

He produced a newspaper from behind his back and handed it to her. "Read the society gossip column." The paper was conveniently opened to that particular section.

Lauren's eyes skimmed over the events of the town's rich and famous. She gave Parker a puzzled frown and caught him trying to peer around the door. "What's this got to do with me?"

"Last paragraph."

As she began to read, a knot formed in her stomach.

The normally calm Swedish-embassy party experienced fireworks when catering king Donald Blake and his fiancée had a row, ending up with the couple's split. Several witnesses said that the violent conversation drew a crowd onto the balcony. It was reported that Lauren Michaels was the one to call quits to their engagement.

Lauren sighed and handed back the newspaper to Parker.

"I take it this little tidbit is true?" Parker said.

"Yes."

"What happened, Lauren? You seemed so happy with Donald."

She wasn't up to this skirmish this morning. Nor was she interested in explaining herself to Parker. "I appreciate your concern, but I'm too upset to talk about it now." She could see his determination to get an answer from her. Resting her hand on his arm, she said, "Thank you for being a friend, Parker. But I need some time to put things in perspective. Don't worry. I'll call you in a few days and we'll talk."

"You're sure?"

"Positive."

Speculation colored his eyes. "All right. If you need me, just call."

She forced a smile. "I will." Closing the door, she rested her head on it.

"Do you think he suspects something?" came Jon's soft voice from behind her.

She faced him. He was leaning on his cane, his eyes bloodshot and his chin rough with stubble. "I don't know. Parker has helped me a lot through the years. I don't know why his concern wouldn't be genuine."

Rubbing the back of his neck, Jon shook his head. "Unless there's something more going on here than we know about. And I don't like the smell of it one bit."

Her stomach growled. She hadn't eaten anything last night and was used to eating her breakfast around seven. She pushed past him and made her way to the kitchen. Jon followed.

"I hope you have something other than blue cornmeal," he grumbled.

She glanced over her shoulder. "I left that treasure at Jimmy's."

"I now know that heaven's looking out for me."

"Beggars can't be choosers, as my Aunt Milly was so fond of telling me."

Jon had always loved French toast, and Lauren decided she'd make that and see if he mentioned anything. It was silly to test him this way, after what they had experienced last night, but her heart needed the reinforcing proof.

She pulled the eggs and butter out of the refrigerator, then retrieved the bread from the bread box.

"Is there anything I can do?" he asked, peering over her shoulder.

"Fill the teakettle with water and set it on the stove. Then you can set the table."

"I don't know where the dishes are."

"I thought you'd gone through the flat with a fine-tooth comb?" She broke an egg over a plate. "I know you've thoroughly gone through my drawers." Her fingers froze over the plate when she heard what she'd said.

He brushed a kiss across her cheek, then smiled. He offered no other comment but whistled as he searched her cabinets for the correct dishes and cups.

When the French toast was ready, she placed the platter on the table, along with syrup and butter. He poured them cups of tea, then sat down.

"You made my favorite," he said, helping himself to several slices.

Her eyes fluttered closed with relief.

Jon immediately noticed her reaction. He looked down at his breakfast, then at Lauren. Would the damn tests never end? He thought they'd put this issue to rest last night. "This was a test, wasn't it, Lauren?" His words were terse.

Her eyes popped open, and her cheeks turned pink. She tried to appear nonchalant as she lifted one shoulder, but he saw the tension in her body. "I didn't set out to make it a test."

He didn't buy her answer.

"But maybe unconsciously I did."

The sternness in his gaze turned to disillusionment. "No matter how many tests you come up with, I'll pass because I'm telling you the truth."

The delight of eating her French toast turned sour. It was apparent that he had a long way to go with Lauren. The battle would be for inches, not big stretches of territory. But he could worry about that later. Right now they had bigger problems. A new one being Parker and his "concern."

It was odd. The entire time he'd known Parker, he never struck Jon as a man concerned with other people's feelings. Oh, he had been sociable and friendly, but no one in London station could call Parker his best friend. Why suddenly had Parker shown sensitivity to Lauren? To be sure, she was a woman who brought out the protective instinct in a man, but was there more?

"Tell me about your friendship with Parker," he said quietly. Yet in spite of the softness of his tone, Lauren jumped.

"He was a rock after I buried you—uh, the body." Her fingers traced the rim of her cup. "He checked up on me every couple of days. Brought me dinner. Listened to me when I got maudlin."

"Has his concern ever seemed forced? Or maybe less than genuine?"

"No." He helped her as she gathered the plates and took them to the sink.

Logically everything in the relationship seemed aboveboard. But Jon's gut was screaming at him to use caution. He glanced down at Lauren's bent head. Her kimono had worked loose, and the delicate skin of her shoulder peeked out at him. He wanted to lean down and kiss it, but he was sure she wouldn't allow it.

What was wrong with him? Why couldn't he think clearly? Hormones, he told himself. The sad thing was he found it harder to concentrate when he was parted from her. Worry over her safety eclipsed everything else.

In addition to his growing concentration problems, there was the new theft at the NATO contractor and the stolen radar system staring him in the face.

With all these dangling ends, he wanted to retreat into himself and figure out what was going on. What he really needed was some uninterrupted time, free of worry.

"Lauren, we need to get away for a while."

She opened her mouth to argue, but he held up his hand, forestalling her.

"I know you don't want to leave your restaurant, but there has been another theft. When I talked to Diamond, he told me about it. He also discovered one of the ways the latest rash of burglaries are tied together." Quickly he explained about the radar system.

"How will me staying away from my restaurant help?" She handed him one of the plates she'd just washed. "Here, dry this."

Snatching the towel from the rack over the sink, he dried the dish. What was the best way to tell her this? "The way it will help is it will allow me to concentrate."

Her hands stilled in the water. She didn't look at him, but a ghost of a smile played around her mouth. "How?"

He couldn't imagine James Bond having this trouble.

"I won't have to worry about your safety. Last night I couldn't keep my mind on the computer files because I kept thinking about you, worrying about what was happening, wondering if you were okay. If you come with me, it will solve that problem. I know you'll be safe."

She didn't respond.

"Besides, you've got a sharp mind, and I need all the help I can get." He placed his fingers under her chin and turned her to face him. "Two days. That's all I ask."

"Where would we go?"

"Somewhere in the countryside. Do you remember that little inn in Exeter? We spent the first night of our honeymoon there on the way to the cottage in Ayr. We could go there."

She worried her bottom lip with her teeth as she considered his plan. "Okay."

His lips brushed over hers. "Thanks, *lieveling.*" He realized that the endearment only slipped out when his emotional guard was down and his heart was naked before her. He needed to tell her that. But later, when they were safe.

Chapter 10

The sign on the side of the road told Lauren that Exeter was eight kilometers ahead. She shifted behind the steering wheel. The little Ford Escort she had rented at Jon's request drove much better than her '72 MG. But any vehicle you could put into motion drove better than her car. And was more dependable.

The closer they got to their final destination, the more tense she became. The thought of spending two days cooped up in a room with Jon made beads of sweat pop out on her upper lip. And if that wasn't bad enough, she'd agreed to go back to the very room where she and Jon had spent the first night of their honeymoon. So in addition to fighting her current attraction, she would be battling sweet memories of the past.

She glanced over at Jon. Clean shaven, sporting sunglasses and a tam covering his hair, the man sitting next to her barely resembled the picture of him that had appeared in the newspaper several days ago. The only thing that would give him away was his cane.

On the back seat lay the laptop. Amazingly Jon had brought the computer with him last night to her flat. In the midst of his "said concern" and worry about her, he was clearheaded enough to bring it with him.

"I find it amazing that you brought the laptop with you to my flat."

His gaze settled on her. "It's just an ingrained habit. One of those spy things—bring the evidence with you in case you can't go back to pick it up."

It hit her then that in one very important way Jon and Donald were very much alike. Their jobs came first; she was second in their lives.

Jon's hand settled on her shoulder, jerking Lauren out of her mental wandering. "You have that look in your eyes, Lauren, that says something is troubling you. What is it?"

The more she thought about it, the more convinced she was that the man was psychic. And the more he was with her, the more accurately he read her mind.

"We should've called the inn and made sure they had room for us."

His fingers brushed a stray strand of hair behind her ear, causing shivers to race over her skin. "If they don't, I'm sure we'll find something in or around the city. What's important is that we get away from London. Don't worry." He continued to stroke the sensitive skin behind her ear. Her breathing became shallow, and her nipples tightened.

"What are we going to use for money?" she asked, grasping at straws.

"Remember when I had you stop by that little park off of Warrington Crescent?"

She nodded.

"Well, that's where I have my dead drop." She frowned at him. "A dead drop is where cash and instructions are left for an agent. Usually dead drops are found in unfriendly countries. Because I was undercover, Diamond and I arranged a dead drop for me for just such an occasion as this. I have plenty of cash."

"Oh." After several minutes of trying to concentrate on the road ahead, she said, "I'm not sure that I will be much help to you."

"You'd be surprised. You have a sharp, analytical mind. And that's what I need right now. Someone I can trust who will look at these files with a fresh eye. Analyze them and maybe see a common thread among them that I've been missing."

The pleasure his words brought washed through her, making her realize how dangerous Jon could be. With a few simple words he had effectively buried her fears of being closeted in a room with him for hours on end.

"Stop there." He pointed to a phone booth beside a small petrol station. "I need to call my boss and let him know where I am. I don't want him to call your cook's flat and get Jimmy."

She pulled off the road and parked by the booth. It took only a few minutes and he was back in the car.

"I left a message. He wasn't there. I'll contact him later."

Her worry about the availability of the room proved groundless several minutes later when they pulled into Exeter and discovered the inn had several open rooms. Jon asked for number 5, the room they'd shared on their honeymoon. It was occupied, so they had to take a room on the second floor.

After eating in the dining room, they went to their room, settled on the love seat and began to work. Jon brought up the directory of the files.

"All right, there are eight companies that have had NATO-related equipment stolen from them over the past five years, plus the codes stolen from a NATO base in Germany. The companies are in different countries—Belgium, France, England, Scotland and Ireland. Orley Inc., Simon-Ray Manufacturers, Engles Tool and finally Jensen Brothers, which had the latest theft, are the four contractors involved with the radar system."

"Were all the thefts bunched together or spread out over time?"

He had to admire how sharp her mind was. "They've been spread out one every six to eight months. When my accident happened, a year passed without any incidents."

"The burglaries of the radar system—over what period of time did they occur?"

"We don't know. The first theft was discovered the day after. That happened three months ago. The second wasn't discovered until they started to ship their product to Teltex, where the system was to be assembled. The third was discovered within a week. That theft happened six weeks ago. The last one was reported after Tony's death."

He glanced down at her. This close, he could smell the soft perfume she wore. It went through him like lightning through the clouds. As far as he was concerned, she smelled even better when her skin was damp with moisture from their lovemaking.

Rein it in, he cautioned himself. They were here to concentrate on the spy ring, not to see how many different ways he could come up with to make love. It didn't help his libido that she had unpinned her hair. It now lay around her shoulders like a dark, mysterious curtain, begging his fingers to sift through the soft, dark strands.

"You didn't know until Diamond told you that the parts were components of a new low-level radar system?"

His gazed fastened on her mouth. Damn, this was going to be harder than he imagined. "No. And that's what's so frustrating. If the guys in ONI—"

"ONI? What's that?"

"Office of Naval Intelligence. If they suspected their system was being snatched, why didn't they alert us at CIA? Of course, Tony and I were trying to figure out why these odd pieces of equipment were being stolen and had begun to question if they were a part of a bigger system. The manufacturers didn't know. All they knew was that they were to produce twenty of their individual items, then ship them to Teltex."

Surprise lit her features. "You spy people don't talk to each other?"

He shook his head.

"But why? It would seem logical for you all to pool your information to do the best job."

"Territory and power, that's what it all comes down to, sweetheart. The greater good gets lost in the individual lust for power."

He ran his fingers through his hair. The first time he had encountered the problem of one intelligence agency holding back information from another he had gone ballistic. Because military intelligence hadn't told him his source in Hungary was dirty, Jon had sent a man into Budapest to collect some information on the Soviets' progress in their version of Star Wars. His man had been captured and, he later found out, killed after hours of torture.

When he discovered by accident that military intelligence knew about his contact and hadn't warned him he searched out the name of the SOB who'd held back the knowledge, found him eating at a chic restaurant in the middle of Georgetown and punched him out. Busting the guy's lip had brought him little satisfaction, but he'd been a lot wiser since then.

"What are you thinking about?" Her voice was filled with concern.

It didn't surprise him that she had guessed correctly that he was reliving past tragedies. What did surprise him was that he wanted to tell her about the treachery and deceit. But if he did that, he'd only dirty her world. His hand cupped her chin, and his mouth settled on hers with an urgency that went beyond wanting to escape the memories. He wanted to lose himself in her welcoming heat and find the peace and oblivion only she brought.

Lauren broke off the kiss. She swallowed and focused her gaze on the computer screen. "We won't accomplish anything by doing that."

His mouth brushed her ear. "Ah, *lieveling,* we'll accomplish a great deal."

As if a spring from the love seat popped through the fabric, she jumped to her feet and glared down at him. "Not what we intended."

He wanted to tell her it was exactly what he intended when he suggested earlier today that they get away from London. But he knew that would please her as much as suggesting a Chicago Cubs fan root for the White Sox.

"You're right," he acknowledged. "We are here to examine these files."

She gave him a speculative look, as if she doubted his sincerity.

"I'll give it my best shot, Lauren. That's all I can promise." It was his honesty about trying—instead of an ironclad promise—that probably won her over. She walked back to the love seat and sat down.

"So there are eight companies that have had NATO equipment stolen. And with the exception of the four with radar system components, you can't find a common link? Was it the same type of equipment that was stolen each time?"

"No. It's been a varied lot. It's like NATO's a superstore and the mole is taking orders."

The old frustration rose up in him. One he'd been feeling since he woke up in the hospital and knew he'd been sold out by someone on his side. "I'm overlooking the link." He pounded his fist on the coffee table. "I know it's there, but I just can't see it. Anthony found it, and so will I."

"I know you will," she softly replied. There was a confidence in her words that eased his mind. Odd, Lauren could always manage to help him see things clearer and let go of thoughts and feelings that he held on to for too long. And that was one of the reasons he was determined to fight for her love.

"You want to see each of the individual files?"

"Might as well."

They went through each of the files, noting the items stolen. Jon had no problem letting Lauren read the files. He trusted her. Trusted her as much as he trusted anyone he'd ever worked with.

The afternoon sped by as they reviewed the records. Finally, after they reviewed the last one, Lauren sat back and closed her eyes. She'd taken notes, jotting down what had impressed her in each file.

"Did you see a pattern that I haven't?" Jon asked.

She shook her head, never bothering to open her eyes. Several strands of hair fell across her cheek. Unable to stop himself, he soothed her hair back. Her eyes slowly opened, and deep within their depths he saw a passion that mirrored his.

His body's reaction was immediate and basic, but this time he didn't act on it. He wanted her to see that although she could make him hard and wanting in an instant, he wouldn't act on it.

"Why don't we eat and let our mind digest what we've just read. Maybe we'll come up with something."

The tension in her muscles drained away. Perversely her reaction annoyed him. She hadn't seemed to have an aversion to kissing him last night.

"Sounds good." She even sounded relieved.

They ate in the dining room of the inn. It was dark and cozy with few people to see them. After the meal Lauren seemed reluctant to go back to the room.

"I know it sounds ridiculous, but could we go for a walk?" she asked. "We've been cooped up in that room for hours. I think the fresh air might help me clear out the cobwebs in my brain."

He glanced out the window and saw the gathering shadows of night. "Sure. Let me get something in the room."

Lauren was surprised he agreed so easily. She thought he would argue against the wisdom of being seen out on the street. She was thankful he hadn't.

What was he getting? she wondered. She shrugged and stared out into the quiet street, grateful for the brief respite. Being with Jon constantly, in such close quarters, was sapping her resolve.

Last night as she lay alone in her bed, knowing Jon was in the other room, Lauren decided that it would be plain stupid to make love to him again before she could sort out the jumble of feelings knotted around her heart.

She meant what she'd said to him last night. She'd trust him with her safety, trust him in all the decisions they had to make to get themselves out of this mess. But at this point she wasn't willing to open her heart to him and let him inside.

What was going to happen after all this mess was finished? Would Jon want to resume their life together? And if he did, could she go along with that decision? If they got back together, would Jon happily go about his life as a spy or would he quit the CIA? Or would he tell her that he was quitting, but then continue in the spy business?

The issue that nagged at Lauren the most was *since Jon had lied to her about his job, had he lied about other things?* What about all those times they had made love, then afterward talked softly of their future, their children, their goals? Had he meant what he said, or had he told her what she wanted to hear?

But the question that cut the deepest was *had he truly loved her or was she simply a convenient body?*

They were all questions that needed to be answered before she would open herself up to him again. It had nearly killed her the first time he'd been taken away from her. She didn't know if she would survive a second round.

But being with him every second of every minute of every hour, feeling the warmth of his large body, having his arm or leg brush against her, was making her body rebel against her brain. Her flesh wanted to be held by him, kissed and caressed, and didn't much care that she'd resolved not to give in to her body's urgings.

"You ready?"

She turned and saw him standing before the stairs. He'd put on his tweed sport coat, and his tam covered his hair. Over his arm he carried her sweater.

"Where's your cane?" she asked, taking the sweater and putting it on.

"You'll have to fill in on our walk." He grasped her arm.

She started to protest, but he shook his head. He hooked her arm around his and urged her out into the night. Once they were halfway down the street, he explained, "A man and woman walking together as lovers wouldn't cause people to stop and stare. Neither will they remember anything unusual about us. If, on the other hand, I'm using my cane, someone might remember."

"Do you think someone might come looking for us?" The thought alarmed her.

He pressed her arm tighter to his chest. "Lauren, nothing has been as I've expected it for a long time. I'm not going to take any chances. Not with you."

"But I don't see how anyone could know where we are."

"I've learned to be prepared for the worst, because it might happen."

It was not a hopeful statement, but bleak and sad and, she sensed, full of memories.

They walked quietly arm in arm down the peaceful street. The houses on either side were straight out of a picture postcard with neatly trimmed gardens, freshly painted fences, window boxes full of flowers. A few windows were lighted, spilling their soft light onto the sidewalk. In the midst of this tranquil scene, Lauren was painfully aware of the man walking beside her. He didn't lean heavily on her, but the slight pressure he put on her arm for balance burrowed into her heart.

"Why didn't you ever write that mystery?" His words in the still night startled her. "You were so eager to do it."

He was again probing into her heart, trying to reach around the emotional wall she was rebuilding. She shrugged.

Stopping, he cupped her shoulders. "What happened, sweetheart?"

He called her sweetheart, not *lieveling*. Like an enlightenment from heaven, it struck Lauren that he only call her *lieveling* when his guard was down and the words were coming straight from his heart without any artifice.

She met his gaze, searching for confirmation of her revelation. "Life got in the way."

His fingers lightly traced her cheek. "Is that a polite way of telling me I'm the reason you didn't pursue your dream?"

He'd nailed it again. It was almost useless to try to hide anything from him or couch her answers in glib replies. "Your life wasn't any picnic, either, these last three years."

"No, it wasn't," he said, some emotion that she couldn't name darkening his eyes. He pulled her arm through his again and started back to the inn.

He stopped in the lobby. "I need to make another call. Why don't you go up to the room? I'll be fine without my cane from here."

As Lauren climbed the stairs, she was again reminded that Jonathan Michaels was first and foremost
a spy. And that meant he knew how to keep secrets.
Something she didn't want from a mate.

The man drummed his fingers on the desk. "Have
you discovered where she is?" he asked Parker.

"No." Parker didn't like the look in the other man's
eyes. "She was there this morning at ten. I went to her
flat under the pretext of asking how she felt after her
breakup with Donald. She seemed upset and said she
wanted to be alone to think."

"So you left her?"

"There wasn't much I could do and not make her
suspicious." Parker paced before the large desk. "I
mean, I couldn't barge into her apartment and demand
that she tell me if she knew where Greg Williams was."

"So where the hell is she at this moment?"

Parker flinched at the other man's deadly, cold tone.
"I don't know. I checked her restaurant. She's been
there every day since she recovered from her husband's
death. Nothing has kept her away."

"So why do you think she's missing now? Do you
think Greg Williams made the connection between the
thefts?"

He shook his head. "Even the inventor doesn't know
how the system was split up."

"But our little Texas girl saw my shopping list.
Maybe she and Greg Williams put it together."

"How?" Parker sat in the overstuffed wing chair.
"Only ONI knew where the parts were, and the only
guy here in London who knew that information was Ted
Anderson. He doesn't remember me studying his plans,

because he was passed out from the drug I gave him. He thought he'd come down with a bad case of the flu.''

The fingers tapped an ominous rhythm on the desk. ''Our profitable days may be at an end if we don't eliminate Greg Williams. He hasn't made you yet, but I think the longer he's out there, the better his chances are of fingering you.''

''So how am I to discover where he is?''

''I think the way to get to him is through Lauren.''

''What's your plan?''

A deadly smile curved the man's lips. ''We harm her baby. A kitchen fire will flush our Lauren out. And when she surfaces, I'll bet Greg will soon follow.''

''Where are you?'' Diamond asked.

''The Black Horse Inn, Exeter. Did you find out any information about Alfred Fox?''

''Yes. He's an English scientist who teaches at the University of Glasgow and works for Teltex. Their research labs are there.''

''Teltex. That file was clean but I think part of it was missing from the disk you sent.''

''I copied those files straight off the embassy computer.''

''Which means, I think, our mole got to the information before you sent it. Damn.'' Where did they go now? ''Maybe I could talk to the professor and get some information. What's his address?''

''He's on vacation in New Zealand but he was due back today.''

''It's worth a try.''

Diamond gave him the Glasgow address.

''Who in the Office of Naval Intelligence decided to parcel out each part of the system?'' Jon asked.

"I knew you were going to ask that."

"Our leak might be there."

A deep sigh rumbled out of Diamond's throat. "I'll have to call in several promises to discover that."

"But you can do it. I have another question relating to the radar system. Do you know what part each manufacturer got?" Something told Jon that piece of information was important.

"Let me see." Jon heard the rustle of papers. "Here it is. Orley had the base. Simon-Ray had the trigger. Engles Tool had what was termed 'the red,' and finally Jensen Brothers had the code."

Jon visualized the list and each component. "Okay. I'll call tomorrow when I get to Glasgow. See if you can pave the way for me to talk to the professor."

As Jon climbed the stairs to the room, he wondered if the guy in ONI might be their leak. Before he'd been reassigned to London, he and Diamond had checked out the personnel at the embassy. In the CIA section, five people, Parker among them, were the same as when he was there three years ago. Four new people had come with him in the new rotation.

On that fateful day three years ago, Jon had signed out, stating only that he was meeting Bright Eyes. Anyone in the department could have read the sign-out sheet. But to discover where he was going, they would've had to talk to the communications officer to see if a neutral third party had been contacted to arrange a meeting place. Unfortunately the communications officer who had sent the message died in a car accident two weeks after Jon had his near fatal accident. That left him and Diamond shooting in the dark, wondering if any of the five men had talked to the communications officer.

But Jon didn't believe any of them was the mastermind behind the ROSES spy ring. They were all too mild-mannered and "proper." That's why he thought the guy in ONI might be their man.

He paused at the top of the stairs. His legs were throbbing with the effort it took to climb a simple flight of steps. He struggled down the hall, grateful there were no witnesses to see his limp. Stopping before his and Lauren's room, he knocked softly. Immediately the door opened.

"Was your boss in?" Lauren asked once he was inside. "And what did he tell you?"

Jon sat on the love seat and began to knead his aching knee. "The man who invented the system lives in Glasgow. He's been off in New Zealand vacationing but was due back today. I think it would be worth our while to go question him. We could drive there—"

The muscle in his thigh contracted into a tight ball. He gritted his teeth against the pain as his fingers dug into the muscle. "Damn leg," he grumbled.

"Let me," she said, kneeling before him. Gently brushing away his hands, she began to knead his thigh. Jon didn't know if it was more pain or pleasure to have her hands on him. And there was definitely a lot of pain.

Finally, after what seemed like hours, the muscle relaxed. His head rolled back on the couch cushions. Her fingers stilled.

"Are you all right?" Her voice was like chimes on the wind.

The heat from her palms seeped through the fabric of his pants, firing his already smoldering desire into a roaring flame. He placed his hand over one of hers. She went still, suddenly aware, he was sure, of the position of her fingers high on his thigh.

"If you're asking if I survived the cramp, I did. If you're asking if I'll survive having your hands on me, the answer is no. I'll die a happy man."

She tried to jerk her captured hand free, but he wouldn't release her. He opened his eyes, and his free hand caught her chin.

"Lauren, *lieveling,* I want you. I want to bury myself in your warmth and have it drive away the chill from my soul."

"Don't do this to me, Jon," she whispered brokenly.

"Why, Lauren? Why?"

"You know why."

Indeed he did. He knew that there were hurts and issues that she wanted resolved. But he also knew that the bond between them had been weakened by what had occurred. That bond needed to be strengthened if they were going to make it. She was his, dammit, and he'd use any means, do anything to make sure it stayed that way.

His knuckles brushed over her cheek. "When I make love to you, I know that there is still hope and beauty in this world." She needed words, so he'd give them to her. He leaned forward, bringing his mouth inches from hers. "But more than that, I want to give you a taste of paradise that I experience each time we are together."

A moan emerged from her throat, and she closed her eyes. At that instant he knew she'd surrendered to him, but he didn't like the feel of this victory, didn't want to think about the underhanded method he'd used to win her. Instead, his mouth covered hers, devouring hers, as if he were a starving man tasting his first food.

His tongue invaded her mouth, dueling with hers, caressing the slick inside surfaces. Her fingers dug into his arms, trying to draw him closer. He pulled her up onto the sofa and over him as he lay back.

He searched her eyes, looking for confirmation that she wanted this as much as he did and found an answering hunger in her. "Do you want this?" he asked, his voice dark with desire.

Lauren felt every inch of his hard frame under hers. The resolve that she had worked so hard to build melted under the heat of his touch. The pull of her flesh was stronger than the pull of her brain.

"Do you want this?" he asked again.

She realized that he wasn't going to allow her to claim afterward that he had coerced her. He may have thought he had outmaneuvered her, but Lauren knew that although her body wanted this, she didn't have to lay her heart open to him. She could divorce that part of her from this lovemaking. "Yes."

His mouth captured hers, pulling her down into his churning passion. Somehow her blouse and bra disappeared, and his shirt was opened so her tender breasts were pressed into the soft hair of his chest.

His kisses demolished the last of her resolve, and she plunged gladly into the world of feeling that he offered.

"I'm not going to make it to the bed," he whispered in her ear.

"Then we'll have to make do here, won't we?" she answered, releasing him from his pants. He didn't bother trying to take her skirt off. Instead, he reached underneath and pulled her panties down her legs. When he entered her, Lauren felt every nerve in her body cry out in delight.

His eyes locked with hers as he began to move with her. When she reached the heights and shattered into a million color-filled pieces, he was with her.

She collapsed on his chest. Listening to the rapid beating of his heart, Lauren realized that she'd been dead wrong. She couldn't divorce her heart from her body.

Chapter 11

Jon's hand lightly caressed the skin of Lauren's back. "Why did you try to keep part of yourself from me?" he softly asked.

She wasn't ready to face this just yet. "What are you talking about?"

He pulled away from her and gazed down into her eyes. "I take back what I've said. You'd make a lousy spy, because you can't lie worth a damn."

She scrambled off him and reached for her blouse. He captured her wrist, stopping her.

"Why, Lauren? Why did you do it?"

"I was only trying to follow your lead. After all, we've made love countless times before, yet you kept a part of yourself hidden from me. Never once, Jon, did you give your entire self to me." A sob caught in her throat. "So you have no reason to complain when I try to do the same thing. The only difference between us was I wasn't successful."

He released her wrist, and she pulled her blouse modestly across her chest.

"How did *you* do it, Jon? How did you keep a part of *yourself* locked away from *me?*"

He pulled back as if she'd slapped him. He zipped his pants and reached for his shirt but encountered her panties instead. He handed them to her.

"Why don't you take a shower while I'm gone, then go on to bed," he said, retrieving his shirt.

"Where are you going?"

His gaze clashed with hers. "I don't know."

The pain from the wound he just opened caused her to gasp. Something flashed in his eyes. It could've been regret. He didn't stay long enough for her to know. Grabbing his cane, he silently left the room. When the door clicked closed behind him, Lauren gave in to the tears clogging her throat.

How could anything so beautiful and earth-shattering disappear so quickly? And how had things disintegrated so fast?

He'd been right in his accusation. She had tried to be dishonest with him, as well as with herself. She'd been trying to live by another's standard, and it hadn't worked. A bitter laugh escaped her lips. *Hadn't worked* was a bit of an understatement. *Miserable failure* more accurately described it.

On wooden legs she walked to the bathroom. As she stood under the spray of hot water, Lauren realized that if she was going to survive emotionally, she would have to stop playing games and be honest—with herself, with Jon. That meant risking her heart. Could she do it? She honestly didn't know.

* * *

Jon stared down into the tankard of ale on the table before him. He certainly had made of mess of things, hadn't he? Of all the dumb things, being speared with his own question ranked right up at the top.

He remembered her saying this morning that she no longer trusted him with her heart. That's why, when he knew she was trying to keep her heart uninvolved, he had poured all of himself into their lovemaking.

Taking a large swallow of the bitter brew, he thought it ironic that in trying to ensure she held nothing of herself back, he gave his all. And when Lauren got around to thinking about what just passed between them, she'd discover he hadn't held anything back.

His blunder had come when he put his anger into words. But her actions had enraged him. What he should've done was keep his stupid mouth shut. Now all he had were fresh wounds he'd inflicted on himself and Lauren. It was a rotten way to end the night.

"Are you wanting another drink before I close the bar?" the bartender asked him.

More alcohol wouldn't change a thing. All it would do was dull his reflexes, and he was in enough hot water now to boil off his skin. "No."

He downed the last of the ale and headed back to the room. Again his leg protested when he climbed the stairs. He paused on the top step, evaluating his performance over the last few days. It was sloppy. He was losing his edge and letting his heart control his head. If he kept it up, it wouldn't be long before he made a serious blunder and innocent people would probably pay for his mistake.

As he unlocked the door to their room, the thought occurred to him yet again that maybe it was time to quit.

Lauren heard the key in the lock. She tensed as the door swung open. After showering and slipping into her gown and robe, she had decided that it would be best for all if she slept on the love seat. She'd pulled the pillow and bedspread from the bed and curled up on the love seat with them. She'd left the lamp on the nightstand burning.

"Lauren?" There was a note of alarm in his quiet voice. "Lauren, where are you?"

She sat up. "I'm here."

His shoulders slumped in relief. "What are you doing over there?"

"Sleeping."

The subtle change in his posture warned Lauren of his coming anger. "Get back in bed." His words were so hard and cold that they could've cut diamonds.

Suddenly her earlier actions seemed childish, and she wanted to explain them to him. "I thought that it might make things easier."

"Get in bed, Lauren. I might be an idiot, but I'm not a rapist."

A wealth of hurt lay buried in his words, and Lauren couldn't ignore them. "It wasn't you I was afraid of."

His eyes closed, and he leaned back against the door. "Thank you."

She gathered up the pillow and bedspread and padded across the room. The bulky spread caught her foot, and she stumbled sideways. Jon stepped forward and tried to steady her, but he stepped out on his bad leg. She heard him curse as his knee gave out, and they both stumbled into the mattress. They landed in a jumble of arms and legs.

Lauren stared into his dazed eyes. This falling together was becoming a real ''thing'' with them. Suddenly it seemed hilarious to her. ''At least we didn't end up on the floor this time,'' she said, trying to hold back her chuckles.

His mouth twitched. She gave him an answering grin. Then a giggle escaped her lips.

''I guess my technique isn't quite as polished as it used to be,'' he said.

''But it gets my attention in a very efficient manner,'' she answered between laughs.

''Yeah, but it's murder on my ribs.''

After their laughter died down, he threaded his fingers through hers and brought her hand to his lips.

''Lauren, I—''

Suddenly she didn't want to hear what he had to say. She feared his words. Her heart couldn't take any more disappointment or disillusionment. ''Don't, Jon.'' She laid her fingers across his mouth to stop his words. ''There will be time enough tomorrow to say what we need to.''

He thought over her proposal, then nodded. Lauren breathed a sigh of relief, but she knew they were simply postponing the moment of reckoning, not eliminating it.

Lauren woke several hours later. She glanced around, wondering what had drawn her from sleep. Jon's side of the bed was empty. Her fingers ran over the place where he had been. The mattress still held the warmth of his body, so he couldn't have left the bed too long ago.

The disturbing thought popped into her brain that after only a couple of days back with Jon, her body was so in tune to his that the lack of his warmth woke her. She was in major-league trouble here.

Scanning the room, she saw Jon sitting on the love seat. He was working on the laptop, and the light from the screen was like a beacon, drawing her. She slipped on her robe and joined him on the love seat.

"What are you doing?" she asked sleepily.

"I wanted to enter the information Diamond told me into the files while I was thinking about it." He glanced at her. "Earlier I got sidetracked."

It was easier to skim over that point. "What information did he give you?"

"You remember the four companies working on the radar system?"

She nodded.

"Well, he gave the individual part that each company produced."

She rested her head on the back of the love seat. "Did it help? Give you any insight?"

"It's been like everything else in this investigation—information that leads nowhere."

"Mmm." Her eyes fluttered closed.

"Go back to bed, Lauren. We've a long way to drive tomorrow."

Her head came up and she stared at him. "Drive?"

"You remember I told you that the professor was due back from his vacation?"

"Vaguely."

"My leg cramped and—"

"Oh, yeah, I remember."

"Dr. Alfred Fox might be our best lead in tracking down the mole. It's worth us driving to Glasgow and talking to him."

"Are you going to let me drive?" she asked.

"I'd better. You're the only one with a valid driver's license. There's no reason to get hauled to jail over a simple thing like that."

They arrived in Glasgow well past nine in the evening. The drive had been long and slow with a wreck on the M5 just outside Bristol and the detour around Carlisle. When they arrived in Glasgow, Jon called Diamond from a phone booth.

"Were you able to set up a meeting with Dr. Fox?"

"Yeah, and it cost me all my markers. Dr. Fox is expecting you. Use your P.I. cover. Mention the Jensen Brothers, and he'll know it's okay to talk to you. Also, the professor knows about the thefts."

"Thanks. I'll be in contact soon."

Jon hurried back to the car and they drove to Dr. Fox's house.

"I want you to wait in the car," Jon told Lauren.

"Why?"

"Because I've got a plausible cover story for me. I don't have one for you."

She pursed her lips, and her fingers tapped on the steering wheel. "All right."

Dr. Alfred Fox was a short man with keen brown eyes shielded by his bifocals. He looked like a man who lived in a world of theory and atoms, as evidenced by the plaid shirt he wore with houndstooth check pants. His wife looked to be no help in the wardrobe department, since she wore a faded housedress with black socks and oxford shoes.

"Dr. Fox, my name is Sam MacKinnon. I've been hired by Jensen Brothers to investigate a theft at their Amsterdam plant a couple of days ago." Jon whipped out an identification card that confirmed he was Sam MacKinnon, private investigator, offices in London and Amsterdam.

The older man gave Jon and his cane a suspicious look. "Who's waiting out in the car for you?"

Just what he didn't need, a curious professor. He was sure that Dr. Fox hadn't been briefed about Lauren. "My wife."

He peered out the door. "What's she doing out there?"

"We were taking a second honeymoon when my company called and asked me to come talk to you. We drove straight from Exeter."

"Have her come in. She must be hungry. The missus would like the company, wouldn't you, Beth?"

Mrs. Fox nodded her head. "I just baked shortbread."

The less people involved, the less chance something would go wrong. But from the stubborn look on the Scotsman's face, Jon knew he didn't have a choice. "I'll get her."

Jon walked out to the car. Lauren rolled down the window when she saw him.

A frown knitted her brow. "What's wrong?"

"Dr. Fox wants you to come inside and have shortbread with his wife."

Lauren's jaw dropped.

"My sentiments exactly. But at this point we don't have a choice." He opened the door for her. "Lauren, we're playing a game here. I need for you to follow my lead. Don't act surprised at anything."

He didn't have time to say anything more because the Foxes were standing on the walkway to their modest house.

Jon stopped and pulled Lauren forward. "Lauren, darling, this is Dr. Alfred Fox and his wife, Beth."

"Oh, my dear Mrs. MacKinnon," Mrs. Fox said, stepping forward. "I'm so sorry that your second honeymoon was interrupted by business. But isn't that the way with men. Always business first, never love."

Jon winced inwardly when Beth called Lauren "Mrs. MacKinnon." Lauren, to her credit, didn't so much as bat an eyelash, but smiled sweetly at the other woman. Lauren was learning much too quickly how to play the game of lie and learn.

"You hit the nail on the head, Mrs. Fox," Lauren replied.

"Call me Beth. And may I call you Lauren?"

"Of course."

Mrs. Fox grasped Lauren's arm. "You men go and talk business. Then join us for tea and shortbread afterward."

Alfred Fox nodded. "Come on, Sam, let's get business out of the way so we can join the ladies for the treat."

Lauren gave Jon a piercing glance. "Yes, Sam, hurry. We still have to find a hotel for the night."

"Oh, Al, we can't let these honeymooners wander around the city looking for a room. We have an extra room. They can stay with us."

Jon didn't know whether he should laugh or cry. It was a dream come true to be able to spend the night at the Foxes and have the run of the place. But he didn't think Lauren would sit still for him slipping out of their room and snooping around. She could be so cranky when it came to spying.

"Thank you, Beth," Jon said. "But I've arranged a surprise for Lauren at a little out-of-the-way inn just north of the city. The Black Boot."

Beth beamed. "Oh, how romantic." She turned to Lauren. "Al and I have been there. It's a wonderful place with cozy little rooms that have fireplaces."

Jon breathed a sigh of relief that he remembered one of the women at the embassy talking about the weekend she and her husband spent at the Black Boot. It usually paid to listen to chitchat around the embassy. One never knew when a stray piece of information would come in handy.

Beth leaned close and in a stage whisper said, "And they have the best stock of Scotch in the entire country. Of course, with your husband, I don't think you'll need anything more to warm your blood."

Lauren's cheeks colored. She gave Jon what others thought was a smoldering look, but in the depths of her eyes, Jon saw her vexation.

Alfred Fox motioned him down the hall. When they entered the study, Al grinned at Jon. "You're a lucky man."

So lucky Jon hoped he would live through it. "Lauren is quite a woman."

Al sat behind his desk. "Now, what is it I can do for you?"

"Jensen Brothers had a theft of a part they were manufacturing for NATO."

"Still, I don't see how I can help you."

"The part was a piece of the radar system you developed for NATO."

The man stood. "I don't know how the radar system was broken up."

"So, once you developed the prototype, you handed it over to NATO officials."

"That's right."

"Where did you develop this prototype? Was it at the university or your office at Teltex?"

"Teltex."

"Could anyone have seen it there?"

He shook his head. "That lab is high security."

"Mind if I see the facility?"

"Tonight? With your wife waiting?"

This was getting more and more complicated.

"I don't think I could get you past the guards this late without prior notice. But tomorrow morning shouldn't be a problem."

Jon wanted to go right now, but it wasn't going to happen. "Could we meet at Teltex at ten tomorrow morning?"

"That's agreeable with me. Now, let's join the ladies."

Lauren set down her toothbrush and rinsed her mouth. After she spit out the water, she raised her head and stared into the mirror. Confusion and turmoil darkened her green eyes, making them appear nearly black in the weak overhead light. Earlier this evening, when Jon had come out to the car and told her to follow his lead, she knew that she'd have to call on her poor acting abilities to get through the meeting. What she hadn't counted on was the Foxes calling Jon "Sam MacKinnon."

Sam MacKinnon. The name of the detective in her mystery, *How Tall Is Red?* Why had Jon used that name? The doubt that had crept into her mind when she watched him easily deceive the Foxes was negated by the use of the fictitious detective's name.

She picked up her toothbrush and toothpaste and headed back to their room. They'd been lucky again with the room; the Black Boot Inn had one left, a cancellation. When she entered the room, Jon was lying in bed, his arms crossed over his chest.

She placed her things in her bag, then slipped off her robe and climbed between the sheets.

"All right, Lauren, tell me what's bothering you," Jon commanded, a tired note in his voice.

It didn't surprise her that he had read her disquiet. He had proved himself time and time again the past few days. "I think you know, Sam."

He sighed and rubbed his hand over his face. "Lauren, the main objective of a spy is to gain information without the party you're spying on knowing that you are doing it."

She pursed her lips. "But Dr. Fox is on our side."

"We think. Besides, I couldn't have walked into his house and said I'm CIA, flashed a badge and asked if he knows—or if he is the one—who is double-crossing us. CIA doesn't issue badges like the FBI. Our main objective is to remain behind the scene and when we go out, we have a cover story. Sam MacKinnon is one of my covers."

"So our government sponsors lying?"

He gave her a piercing look. "You're smarter than that, Lauren. All governments lie. It would be foolish for the U.S. to run around telling the truth, when all the other countries are lying on a daily basis."

Lauren sat up and wrapped her arm around her knee. "No matter who does it, or how many people or nations do it, lying is wrong.'' She turned her head toward him. ''And when you willingly lie, the only one you hurt is yourself.''

His hand stroked down her hair. ''You're right, Lauren. Each time you lie, you lose a little part of yourself. I know.''

''Has it been worth it?''

His expression was sad. ''No.'' He reached up and turned off the lamp.

''Why did you use Sam's name?''

''Do you need to ask?''

''Yes.''

''Because it brought me closer to you.''

Enclosed in the darkness, Jon's aching soul reached out to Lauren. He was hurting, and she couldn't ignore his pain. Her hand groped over the bed until she found his hand. She laced her fingers through his and brought his hand to her lips.

''Lauren.''

It was a call for help. A drowning man grasping for a lifeline. She scooted across the space that separated them and slipped her arm around his waist. Her mouth settled on his, giving to him all the tenderness that was in her heart.

There was nothing tame in Jon's response. His arms clamped around her, and his lips devoured hers. The heat and passion coming off him singed her, but she didn't care. This was right. This was something she could do to fight against the darkness that Jon lived and worked in.

She wrenched her mouth free, then trailed soft kisses down the scar on his cheek. He didn't try to fight her, but instead understood that she wanted to be the one to give this time.

Her hands soothed over his chest. Her fingers traced the scar that curved over his side and ended at his hip. Her lips followed the path of her fingers.

When she reached the end of the scar, Jon's hands grasped her waist.

"I can't take any more." With that, he settled her on himself.

Lauren felt as if she'd been thrust into the heart of a furnace, tongues of flames surrounding her, eating her. She gave in to the consuming heat, crying out her joy. Jon followed her into the inferno.

Afterward, in the ashes of that passion, Lauren felt a new peace.

Jon listened to Lauren's even breathing. His mind still reeled with the power of their lovemaking. He felt Lauren's heart calling to him, pulling him out of the night that he knew so well, calling to a soul that was lost.

He knew Lauren had been upset by the cover story he had used. It had been in every line of her body that the lies bothered her.

What troubled him was Lauren's attitude toward his business. She was a smart enough woman to know that deceit was an integral part of covert work. The question that gnawed at him was *why wouldn't she acknowledge and accept it?* Her problem could be due to the fact that in Lauren's past, she'd been hurt deeply by several stepfathers who'd lied through their teeth and hurt her and her mother.

But if he was honest with himself, he would have to admit that he didn't like involving Lauren in his lies. As a matter of fact, this time his cover hadn't fit as well as it had in the past.

Combined with the other things, Jon knew he was going to have some hard thinking to do about his future.

At ten the next morning, Jon and Lauren met Alfred Fox at the front gate of the Teltex plant. Dr. Fox okayed their passage through the gate and past the guard. He then took them on a tour of the main plant and his lab. Jon couldn't fault the security. It was tight and efficient.

As they were leaving the building, Jon was still puzzling how anyone could have stolen secrets from Teltex. The theft had happened three years ago, but a review of Teltex procedures had concluded that the theft was not an inside job.

"Jon, look." Lauren pointed to a truck parked by a loading dock. "Blake Catering must have the contract for this site."

Like a bolt from the sky, the possibility of how the theft from Teltex occurred came to him. A catering company or other outside contractor. Like another bolt of lightning, he realized that the Teltex file he'd been reviewing made no mention of an outside catering firm holding a contract for an on-site cafeteria. What if *all* the plants that had been burglarized had outside catering companies? What if they all had the *same* catering company?

"Does Blake Catering hold the contract for your cafeteria?" Jon asked Dr. Fox.

"Yes."

"Do you know for how long?"

The older man rubbed his chin. "Let me see, they first came the year I had my gall bladder out. That was—" he scratched the side of his head "—almost four years ago."

Jon shook Dr. Fox's hand. "Thank you, doctor, for all your help."

"What help?"

"I think, doc, you gave me the key to the thefts."

Lauren waited until they were in the car before she asked Jon, "What key did you uncover?"

He leaned over and placed a kiss on her cheek. "It was you who gave me the idea."

Her startled gaze flew to his. "How?" Unfortunately her hands followed her head, and the car veered to the left.

"Whoa." Jon grabbed the wheel and straightened them out.

"Sorry," she murmured.

"Don't worry, sweetheart."

His finger traced down her neck, and that familiar wanting that he called forth sprang to life. "You were going to tell me how I gave you the key to this—" she waved her hand "—situation."

"Tony and I were looking for a common thread that ran through each theft. Well, maybe each of these companies has Blake Catering running their on-site cafeteria. What would be easier than to use the cover of a catering company to gain access to the plant? No one would question you being there. And if they found you there after-hours or in the early-morning hours, you have a logical excuse for being in the building."

She glanced away from the road. "So what are you going to do?"

"I want you to drive us back to the Black Boot and we'll keep the room for another night. Then I'm going to call every one of these companies and see who has their cafeteria contracts."

"And if Blake Catering is the one serving them all?"

"Let's wait and see. One thing I've learned in this business is to go cautiously and never count your chickens before they hatch."

Lauren stared at the list of companies Jon had jotted down on a piece of paper. Blake Catering, or some subsidiary of it, had been the contractor at five of the eight facilities. Also, Blake Catering helped on occasion with NATO functions in Brussels.

What caught her eye was the set of odd notations Jon had made by the last four companies—the ones that had the radar system?

"Base, trigger, red, code." She'd seen that list before, but where?

"Jon, what is this by these companies?" She held up the piece of paper.

He took the list from her. "What?"

"The words that you've scribbled by the last four companies on this list." She pointed it out to him.

"Those are the parts of the radar system that each of those companies manufactured. Why?"

She tapped her lips with her forefinger. "I've seen this list before."

His eyes narrowed. "Where?" Excited tension rolled off him in waves.

It was right there at the edge of her memory, hovering. Where had she seen that odd list? It had been in an unusual— "I know. I saw that list on a piece of paper in the library at the Blake house."

Jon's hands grasped her shoulders. "It was out in the open?"

"No. It was the night of Donald's and my engagement party."

Jon's face clouded over like a spring storm in central Texas.

"Do you want to hear this?"

He nodded.

"As I was saying, that night I was upset. It seems that a man turned up in my apartment claiming to be my dead husband."

His eyes narrowed.

"I didn't feel much like socializing, so I escaped into the library for a few minutes. The light was on at the desk, and I thought someone might be in the room, but when I called out, no one answered. I sat behind the desk and . . . stewed."

A grin tugged at his lips.

"Don't look so smug. Anyway, when I got up to return to the party, I knocked a book off the desk. When I picked up the book, a piece of paper fell out. At first I thought it was just a scrap, but then I saw that list of parts."

"What did you do?"

"I put the paper back in the book and went back to the party."

"Did anyone see you coming out of the library?"

"I don't think so." She tried to recall if she'd seen a person in the hallway. "I didn't run into anyone."

Jon stood and began to pace. "Well, I think our chickens have hatched."

"Meaning you think Blake Catering is involved in this mess."

"Let's check. I bet the three companies where Blake wasn't on-site are the companies that had things stolen en route. Or maybe if we check further, we'll find the people in charge of each cafeteria buy from Blake. Let's look at the files again, then make some calls."

Forty minutes and a half-dozen phone calls later, Jon's theory proved true. Two companies had Blake deliver foodstuffs. The one who had no connection to Blake had had their burglaries occur when the shipments were made.

"This is what Tony must've stumbled across," Jon said. His jaw clenched and his hand knotted into a fist. "Damn, why didn't I think of this sooner? Tony and I had begun to check if any of these companies had some outside contractor, which wasn't listed in the file, in common. He must've make the connection that ROSES was Blake Catering. That was how they could get into highly secure plants."

He stood and began to pace again. "But how did the mole know Tony had stumbled onto their secret?"

"Did he call someone else besides you?" Lauren asked.

Jon's eyes darkened. "I don't know. Maybe."

"Are you sure that it was the mole who killed Tony? Perhaps he called someone at Blake Catering, and that individual killed your partner."

He shook his head. "Tony wouldn't have contacted anyone at Blake before he told me. So that leaves only the mole."

"Do you have any idea who the mole is?" Lauren regretted asking the question instantly. Jon's expression turned fierce, yet there was an underlying emotion of pain that showed in his eyes.

"No. Our traitor or his handler is very smart. After I had my accident, we tried several times to isolate who it was who betrayed me. We sent different people on missions and trips, then fed what was considered sensitive information through the London station. None of the information leaked." He sat beside her. "We reassigned several people and fed information through their new assignments. Again nothing leaked."

Lauren placed her hand on his thigh. She wanted to say something to comfort him, but what?

His hand covered hers. "I got this feeling that the mole is still in London. Wisely all the information that has been compromised over the last three years has had more than one source."

"Who are the people who are the same as when you were here?"

"There are five. Johnson, Dewell, your friend Parker James, Stewart and Allen."

"I can't believe that Parker would be involved in anything like this. Granted, he's been a pest the last week or so. But he's been such a good friend."

Cupping her chin, he raised her gaze to his. "Lauren, remember you didn't have a clue to what I did."

She jerked her head away.

"It would've been the perfect cover for Parker to keep an eye on you by striking up a friendship."

"Do you mean you don't think he simply wanted to help me through a bad time? I wouldn't be worth it?"

"Of course you'd be worth it, but people in the spy field often don't act on their true feelings. We're experts at hiding our true motives."

All color left her face. He'd indicted himself again.

"Dammit, you know what I mean."

"Yes, I do," she answered quietly, turning her face away.

"For that matter," he whispered, "your ex-fiancé might also be a spy."

Lauren's gaze flew to his, her eyes wide with the horror. Jon realized he'd uttered his thoughts out loud.

Suddenly it occurred to Lauren that she'd been surrounded by a tight circle of spies. It was as if she were a lamb tied to a tree for the purpose of luring wolves out in the open so they could be killed. Bait. That's all she was. Bait for the wolves.

Lauren jumped to her feet, fighting the tears that clouded her vision. "Terrific. I'm surrounded by liars and cheats. And it looks like I've been used by every one of you."

Her barb hit its mark, because she saw the muscles of Jon's jaw tighten.

He stood and reached for her, but she stepped away from his touch. "Don't."

She spun around and raced for the door. If she was in the room with Jon an instant longer, she knew she'd say something unforgivable.

Chapter 12

Jon collapsed back onto the couch. It was out of the question for him to try to run after her. Probably as mad as she was at the moment, she'd flatten him if he tried to get near her.

Cradling his head in his hands, he cursed a vivid blue streak. He went through his vocabulary of choice words twice, then threw in every profanity he'd ever heard in a foreign language before his anger subsided enough for him to think clearly. When his mind began to function again, he heard Lauren's words: *I'm surrounded by liars and cheats. And it looks like I've been used by every one of you.*

The words were harder to endure than a beating with a steel pipe because he knew she had purposely included him in that disreputable bunch.

"Think, Michaels," he scolded himself. "You're not going to do her any good by feeling sorry for yourself. Think and figure out what's going on."

After divorcing—or trying to divorce—his feelings from the situation, he considered what she'd said. Did Lauren have a valid point? Had she been used? Had Parker befriended her simply to keep an eye on her? It made sense to Jon. Parker's friendship with Lauren had never sat well with him, rather like trying to cram his size-eleven foot into a size-nine shoe.

And what about Lauren's fiancé, Donald thin-lipped Blake? How did he fit into this tidy little picture? Had Donald purposely set his sights on Lauren to keep her under surveillance? If he had, he was a bigger bastard than Jon thought. And if he had, Jon would make sure the man paid with a great deal of pain.

Jon needed to question Lauren about how she'd met Donald Blake. Together maybe they could pick out the truth in this world of subterfuge.

"Ah, sweetheart, it truly must seem like you've been used by every man in your life," Jon murmured to the empty room.

Although Jon hadn't used her, his conscience was just as black as the other players in this nasty game. He hadn't purposely dragged her into this ugly web, but she seemed to be at the center of it. And it was all attributable to her association with him.

When he'd first appeared in Lauren's apartment, Jon had had the feeling that he'd set something bad in motion. Time had proved that feeling right.

Right now he had another dark premonition, that Lauren was slipping out of his hands. Her heart was drifting away from him. And if he didn't do something quickly, she would be lost to him forever.

* * *

Lauren was so mad that she was surprised she didn't leave a trail of fire behind her as she marched down the street.

The whole lot of them were sorry so-and-sos, and if she never saw any of them again in this lifetime it would be too soon.

Every cotton-picking one had used her. *Everyone except Jon,* her mind whispered.

He might not have used her, but he was the reason she was in this fix. And she was more than willing to lay the responsibility at his feet. If he hadn't been a spy doing his spy thing, her life wouldn't be in the toilet at this moment.

She stopped and took a deep, steadying breath. She couldn't decide whether she wanted to scream out her anger at the top of her lungs or sit down on the sidewalk and bawl her eyes out. Tears began to cloud her vision. And although she wanted to vent her pain and rage, doing it here on the street in the sight of everyone and their Aunt Martha wasn't exactly how she wanted to do it.

Desperate to divert herself, she looked around. In front of her was a bakery. Malcomb and Sons. There was no better way, in her opinion, to soothe ruffled emotions than a good pastry. With a silent prayer of thanks, Lauren opened the bakery-shop door.

After purchasing a half-dozen scones, Lauren walked to the park at the end of the street and sat on the wooden bench. Eagerly she opened the sack and pulled out a scone. With the first bite, she closed her eyes, savoring the buttery taste. If she had some strawberry jam, it would be perfect. Then at least there would be something in her life that was right.

She shied away from that thought, not ready to deal with anything else besides eating at the moment. She was successful in keeping her mind blank while she downed the first scone. Halfway through the second, reality intruded.

The prospect of Donald or his father being a spy was unbelievable. But what did she know? Her husband had been one, was one, and she hadn't known.

Wasn't it ironic that she, who had a nearly obsessive dislike of lies and liars, was surrounded by men who perfected the art?

You've managed to lie quite easily over the last few days, a voice in her head whispered.

"But there hadn't been a choice," she answered. She hadn't liked lying, but she had done it to protect Jon.

It was still lying, Lauren.

The revelation wasn't appreciated.

See how easy it was? Can you condemn Jon when you've done the same?

Glancing at the peaceful park scene, the carpet of grass, bushes clipped into shapes of animals and trees sporting their autumn colors, Lauren wondered if she would ever again experience the feeling of calm that permeated this little corner of the world.

Taking another bite of the scone, she tried to concentrate on the heavenly taste, but her mind kept chasing the troubling thoughts that had driven her from the room.

Parker a spy?

And perhaps Donald a spy, too?

And she was the biggest fool walking the face of the planet.

Maybe all this sinister thinking was wrong. Maybe Parker really had been concerned for her and wanted to help her through a tough time in her life. Maybe Donald had really liked her and wanted to marry her. And maybe the sky is green and there are fairies that roam the countryside.

She swallowed the last piece of the scone, then stared at the white bakery sack in her lap. She'd bought six scones, intending to pig out. But no matter how many scones she ate, it wouldn't change any of the circumstances of her life, and would only add inches to her hips.

As she stood, Lauren considered throwing away the bag. *Jon loves currant scones,* a voice in her head whispered. Lauren reconsidered tossing the bag, but her heart immediately cast aside the petty thought.

Clutching the sack, she started back to the Black Boot Inn. Her life had taken on a surreal quality in the past few days. How had she ended up in this mess?

Well, no matter how she'd gotten here, she needed to face up to it. She wasn't a coward.

Jon looked out the window, searching the street for any signs of Lauren. Glancing at his watch, he noted it had been over an hour since she had stormed out of the room. If she didn't show up in the next five minutes, he was going to go out looking for her.

Into his line of vision walked the very woman who filled his thoughts. Lauren. She had just turned the corner and stopped, staring up at their room. He could just imagine the thoughts going through her brain. He didn't wait to see if she walked away. Instead, he hurried out of the room and down the stairs.

He cursed the stupid steps. He'd climbed enough of these torturous things in the past few days to last him a lifetime. When he reached the bottom, he came face-to-face with Lauren.

"Where are you going?" she asked.

"Out to get you. I didn't know if you were coming back," Jon said, relief flooding his body.

"I considered leaving, but that wouldn't have solved anything." She shoved the bag at him. "Here."

"What's this?" Curious, he opened it. "Currant scones." He glanced up. "You bought these for me?"

She didn't say anything.

Her gesture deeply touched him. "Thank you, sweetheart."

The endearment didn't go down well.

"Lauren, we need to talk about—things."

Her shoulders stiffened. "I know."

They stared at each other for a moment, then she started up the treads. The sight of her gently swaying hips hit him like an arrow from a crossbow.

Keep your mind on the matter at hand, he told himself. *Remember feelings and lust take a back seat to solving the problem.* Reining in his desire, he followed her up the stairs.

Once they were in the room, Lauren walked over to the window and stared out. Jon knew that this conversation was going to be hard, but from her stance, back board-straight, arms folded across her chest, he knew this was going to be harder than talking a Texan out of his boots.

He joined her at the window. "Tell me how you met Donald Blake," he asked, trying to keep his voice soft and mellow.

Her brow arched. "Why do you want to know?"

"I think it might help us to decide who in Blake Catering is working with the mole."

"You mean Parker?"

His hand rubbed over his mouth. "I don't know. Parker's looking more and more like our leak, but it will have to be checked out."

"How?"

"Dammit, Lauren, let's just stick to one jerk at a time. Let's talk about Donald."

Her mouth pulled up into a tight pucker, and her eyes were flashing fire. Great, just what he needed, to annoy her.

He opened his mouth to apologize, but before he could say anything, she spoke. "I'd gone to a restaurant convention in Liverpool. I was looking at commercial ovens, and Donald was looking at refrigerators in the next booth. We started up a conversation and found we had a lot in common. A couple of weeks later, he showed up at my restaurant and asked me out."

"Did he seem overly eager?"

Her stony expression clearly told him that his question didn't strike the chord he wanted.

"What I mean is did anything seem odd or strike you as funny when Donald started asking you out—aside from the fact that he wanted to date you?"

Her chin lowered and her gaze narrowed. "I beg your pardon?"

"Ah, hell—" He threw up his hand. "You know what I mean."

"Yes, I know. There was nothing out of the ordinary. He didn't take off his shoe and dial Control—he didn't disappear beneath the floor of a telephone booth as Maxwell Smart used to in 'Get Smart.'"

He wanted to tell her this wasn't the time for inane comments about old television shows and imaginary spies, but wisely he kept his thoughts to himself. She had enough to deal with at the moment.

"Donald was simply a pleasant man whose company I've enjoyed." She glanced at him as if he were a tree fungus. "And I think he enjoyed mine."

Touching her cheek, he murmured, "I know he did."

She turned her head away from his touch. Jon felt the loss as keenly as if she'd cut off his fingers.

"Was there anyone else who made you feel uncomfortable or who seemed odd?"

She didn't answer right away, but considered his question. "Again nothing out of the ordinary. Donald's father is a nice man and seemed to welcome me into their family." Her fingers ran down the edge of the curtain. "You know the Blakes come from an old, moneyed family. Donald and his father went to all the right boarding schools, then attended Cambridge. They belong to the right clubs in London and travel in the right circles. Marshall, Donald's father, decided he didn't want to simply rest on the family's name and money. So he did the unusual and went into business."

Jon wondered if Marshall's noble gesture of working was born out of the fact that the family found itself out of cash.

Unaware of his speculation, Lauren continued. "Both Donald and his father are a bit reserved. They don't let their feelings hang out like Americans, but I didn't expect anything else from them. In fact, I found their attitude comforting."

Her words startled her, and her gaze flew to his to see if he'd heard her last statement. Unwittingly she had handed him a key, and he wasn't going to let the opportunity pass without using it.

"What do you mean?" he softly asked.

A mulish expression crossed her lovely face, then she looked out the window again.

He brushed the back of his fingers across her cheek. "Tell me what you mean, sweetheart." He pitched his voice low, wanting his tone to seduce her, wanting to pull her heart toward his.

She wrapped her arms tighter around her waist but didn't speak.

Gently he cupped her chin, then slid his hand down her throat, his fingers spread wide. Under his middle finger and thumb, he could feel the rapid beat of her heart. He waited patiently, not moving a muscle and praying that his body would convince hers to yield.

Her eyes fluttered closed, and a sigh slipped from her lips. "It means that I didn't want to feel again the same earth-shattering passion I felt with you." She didn't open her eyes, but kept them closed. "I wanted something safe, something that wouldn't tear me apart if it ended." Her eyes opened. "And I was right. Breaking my engagement to Donald didn't rock my world to its foundation."

It was damn selfish of him, but he was glad that she didn't grieve over the breakup.

"But having you show up did." He heard clearly the despair in her voice.

Her words ripped through his heart like a chain saw through a tree. He leaned his cane against the wall and slipped his arms around her waist, pulling her close. She didn't uncross her arms, which made it awkward to hold her, but he didn't release her.

"Ah, Lauren, I'm sorry. I would've stayed out of your life if I could've."

Her head jerked back, and her elbows came up hitting his arms. "What are you saying?" Her arms dropped to her sides.

"That I didn't mean to cause you pain."

Her eyes turned cold. "Are you telling me that if there hadn't been the chance rumors that you were still alive would surface, you wouldn't have ever bothered to contact me?"

Her tone, icy to the point of bringing pain, told him that if he didn't straighten out her misconceptions in the next few minutes, they wouldn't have a future together.

"No, that's not what I meant at all. I would've waited until the mole was unmasked and it was safe for you."

Some of the ice in her gaze thawed. "Would you have let me marry Donald?"

That was a question he'd wrestled with in the dark hours of the night when he discovered Lauren had begun dating again. Visions of her in the Englishman's arms, making love to him, had nearly driven Jon crazy.

"I don't know."

Disappointment colored her green eyes.

His hand slid up her spine to cup the back of her head. "Everything inside me rebels at the thought of any other male putting his hands on you. You're mine. My woman. My wife. And I think I would've killed Donald on your wedding night before he had a chance to do anything."

He didn't apologize for the primitive feelings running through him. Instead, he gave in to the most basic, and his mouth settled over hers. Apparently Lauren wasn't offended with his show of male aggression. She wrapped her arms around him and opened her mouth for him, welcoming him.

Jon felt as if a volcano suddenly erupted in the middle of Glasgow. The ground under their feet seemed to shift, and a white-hot fire shot up around them.

He pressed her hips into his, and the heat in the room intensified. Wanting her, needing her, consumed him from the inside out. He trailed kisses down her neck to the top of her blouse. As his fingers undid the buttons of her blouse, she worked on the buttons of his shirt.

In a frenzied drive, they discarded their clothes as they moved toward the bed. They tumbled onto the mattress, Lauren landing on top of him. They needed no other foreplay but being as one. She wasn't shy, reveling in his rough thrusting. With one final flex of his hips, he sent them both over the edge, plunging into the fiery ecstasy that was love.

Lauren listened to Jon's heartbeat slow as she came back to the real world. Each time she made love with him, the stronger the tie between them became. And each time they made love, she surrendered a little more of her soul to him.

The question that plagued her like a demon disrupting her peace was what would happen to them once Jon caught his traitor? Would he continue playing spy or would he quit? And if he continued, would she be able to endure watching him leave on his missions without dying a little more each time he left?

She brushed her cheek over the soft hair on his chest. His fingers toyed with a strand of her hair.

"What are you thinking?"

This was the time to ask him. Hadn't he said, in not so many words, that he loved her? His body certainly had said it. But now it was time to see if he loved her more than he did his job.

"I was wondering about our future."

His fingers stilled. "What about it?"

She raised up and braced herself on his chest. "What happens to us when you find your mole? Are you going to continue working for the CIA, going on missions, disappearing for weeks like you did the last time?"

His expression turned hard and remote. "I won't be doing any more fieldwork. My leg assures that."

"So does that mean that you're going to stay with the CIA?"

He looked away from her. "I don't know. I hadn't thought that far ahead."

It wasn't the answer that she wanted. But suddenly Lauren was afraid if she pressed him for an answer, she'd get one that she didn't want to hear, one she couldn't face now.

Instead, she laid her head down on his chest, wanting only to enjoy this moment.

Jon sat in the chair and watched Lauren sleep. It was close to ten, but he didn't have the heart to wake her. He recognized the signs of her emotional exhaustion. She was edgy, tired easily, and her emotions were on a surface level.

Of course, her exhaustion was understandable. Lauren had been plunged into the center of the storm raging between him and the mole. Was their mole Parker? They had funneled decoy information through London Station and nothing had leaked. Whoever was controlling the mole in London was smart enough to know that his man was in danger of being caught and kept his man clean.

It was time to call Diamond. And maybe it was time to check Parker's bank account. Jon walked to the bed and brushed a kiss across Lauren's cheek. Her eyes fluttered open, and a welcoming smile curved her lips.

"Good morning." She stretched like a contented cat. The movement made the bright yellow sheet slide down her body, revealing the top of her breasts. "What time is it?" she drowsily asked.

"It's ten."

The drowsiness left her expression. "Why did you let me sleep so long?"

He sat down beside her and grasped her hand. "You needed the sleep."

Snuggling closer to him, she asked, "What are we going to do today?"

"After I call my boss, I plan to check out Parker's bank account. Maybe I should visit his house, see if he has any expensive hobbies or tastes that he couldn't support on his salary."

She tucked the sheet under her arms and scooted into a sitting position. "Are you going downstairs to call?"

"Yeah. I don't trust hotel phones. Never know who's listening. A phone booth is more secure."

"I'll shower while you're gone."

He leaned over and placed a kiss on her mouth. She moaned and wrapped her arms around his neck. His hand roamed over her back, and he was tempted to slide his hands around her sides and stroke her breasts. But if he did that, he'd never get downstairs. He broke off the kiss and rested his forehead against hers.

"I'd like to finish this but . . ."

She sighed and withdrew her arms. "Go."

He left the room while he still had the will to go. He walked down to the lobby and stepped into the enclosed booth. After dialing, he got Diamond.

"How did your meeting go with Dr. Fox?"

"Good. He was totally charmed by Lauren."

"Maybe you should work as a team."

Everything in Jon rebelled at the thought. Although he had chosen to live in the shadows, Lauren hadn't, and he wouldn't try to seduce her into his darkness. He'd dragged her in far enough as it was. "No."

"What did you learn?"

"Blake Catering was the company that served three of the four plants that were manufacturing the radar system. I checked with the other companies who had had robberies. Blake served a couple of the places, and the ones Blake didn't serve directly, they delivered food to the on-site cafeterias."

"You think this was what Tony stumbled onto?"

"Could be. What I suspect is that they use the catering cover to gain access to the facilities, then they have the run of the place. Our mole is feeding these secrets to Blake Catering."

"Any new leads on who the mole is?"

"I think it's time to start taking a look at people's bank accounts. And Parker James is first on my list."

"Well, I've got news on Parker. The officer in ONI who was responsible for the radar system is Ted Anderson. He's a straight arrow according to his superiors. But after checking personnel records, I discovered Ted Anderson served in the navy with Parker James. They were on the same ship for several tours of duty. Even more interesting, after talking with Ted, I discovered Parker made a trip to Brussels last fall and spent time with Ted. Old friends celebrating Ted's promotion."

Jon cursed. "I had a feeling about Parker, but I kept telling myself it was plain old-fashioned jealousy since he'd struck up a friendship with Lauren."

"We're going to need a little more proof than your gut feeling."

"How about a little trip to Parker's house, see if he's sporting some expensive habits that his salary won't support. Also, there's a bookie friend of mine I'm going to check with to see if he knows anything about Parker."

"All right, but I don't want any Lone Ranger stunts out of you. No charging in without backup. Understand?"

"Yes."

"Keep me updated. I want to catch Parker redhanded, no questions about his guilt."

Once Jon hung up, he felt the first adrenaline rush that came with knowing he was closing in on his target. He'd stop by Davy's before visiting Parker's house. If Parker was betting or gaming, Davy would know it or would know someone who would know. Besides, Davy would be able to get him a gun, and he wasn't going anywhere near Parker without one.

When he entered the room, Lauren was sitting on the bed, dressed and ready to go.

"What's wrong?" she immediately asked.

"We're going back to London. It's time we paid a little visit to Parker James."

Lauren waited until they were in the car before she questioned Jon. When he had entered the room, he had a look in his eyes that told her he was in another universe and it would be a waste of her time to try to get any information out of him. She remembered that particular look from the year they were married. Right before he would go on one of his "trips," Jon would get this particular look in his eyes. No matter how hard she questioned him, all she would get were nods and noncommittal sounds of agreement. Now she knew what that look meant, and she knew that concentration was with him when he started one of his missions. This time she decided to wait, and once he was enclosed in the car with her, she would spring her questions.

They were an hour out of Glasgow, and Jon's gaze had lost some of its intensity, when Lauren asked her first question.

"What did you find out from your boss?"

"Huh?"

It wasn't a promising beginning. "Jon, you went downstairs to call Diamond. What did he tell you?"

Lauren felt him struggle within himself.

"Jon, I think I have a right to know what was said."

He closed his eyes and nodded. "You're right. I guess I've just fallen back into my 'mission mentality.' I'm not used to working with a partner out in the field."

"Quit stalling."

"It seems that Parker knew the ONI officer in charge of the radar system. They were old navy buddies, and Parker just happened to visit his friend around the time the radar system was being parceled out."

"That looks bad for Parker. It could be coincidence. Do you have any proof?"

He fixed her with a hard stare. "This isn't going to go to court, Lauren. Not at this stage."

"But if he is the one doing the spying for the other side, don't you want to be able to put him behind bars?"

"I'll do the right thing."

His answer worried Lauren. Jon's professional persona had emerged, and she knew she didn't want to be on the wrong side of his anger.

"Tonight, I want it done, tonight. Do you have someone lined up to do it?"

"Yes."

"Someone who won't talk if they're caught?"

"I've got an expert, the best torch in the business. Don't worry."

"I always worry, especially with you in charge."

"If I'm so incompetent, why do you use me?"

"It's a question I've been asking myself a great deal lately."

Fear clutched Parker's heart.

It was close to midnight when they arrived on the outskirts of London. Instead of driving to either her flat or Jimmy's, Jon instructed her to turn off the M1 and directed her to a small pool hall in Edgward.

"May I ask why?"

"Because we need to make some inquiries before we take a look at Parker's house." He pointed to the next streetlight. "Turn left there."

"What do you hope to find at Parker's? Surely he wouldn't leave out any sort of incriminating evidence."

"Probably not, but I want to see if Parker is living beyond his means. And if he is, I want to know how he's financing his life-style."

She started to suggest Parker was doing it like everyone else, by credit cards, but she didn't think Jon would appreciate her observation.

"Stop here."

Lauren pulled up in front of a timeworn building that looked as if it had been hit during World War II and no one had bothered to repair it. Two men came barreling out of the front door, followed by a billow of smoke and loud music.

"Come on," Jon said, opening the passenger door.

"What?" she asked, surprised he didn't want her to wait in the car.

"I don't want to leave you alone in the car at this time of night, in front of a pool hall. Besides, Davy will have something for us to eat."

Lauren eyed the place. Whatever Davy had, she didn't know if she wanted any.

Jon pulled Lauren to his side as they entered the hall. Two of the three pool tables had people around them. In the back of the room there stood a bar. Through the smoke, Lauren could make out a tall, large figure. Jon edged his way around the room, Lauren in tow.

When they were close enough for Lauren to actually see the bear of a man, he smiled broadly, revealing a gleaming gold tooth. "Sam, it's good to see you, old friend."

Lauren stiffened at the name. Her husband seemed never to give anyone his true name. She wondered if she really knew it. Jon's arm slipped around her waist, plastering her against his body.

"Davy, the missus and I have had a long drive and need a little something to eat and drink. Think you could provide it?"

"I can. Mavis, watch the bar." He motioned Jon toward a door behind the bar. "This way."

They followed him into a small kitchen that was amazingly clean and well cared for. "I got some Scotch broth and black bread. That do you?"

The thick barley soup made Lauren's mouth water. "Sounds heavenly," she said before thinking.

Jon grinned at her. "You found the way to my missus's heart."

Davy's chest shook with mirth. "I don't think she's looking." He winked at Lauren.

Davy dished up the dinner, then sat down beside them with a mug of ale. "Now, Sam, why are you here?"

"I need to know if an American named Parker James has any bad habits. Women, bookies, gaming halls. He might not be going under his own name. He works at the American embassy. He's five foot eleven, one hundred eighty-five pounds. Brown thinning hair and brown eyes."

Davy stared down into his mug, then up at Jon. "That could describe half the men on the island, 'cept the American part. Anything that would make him stand out in a crowd?"

"No."

"Can't say I know the gent. But my clientele is small-time. I could check around."

"How long would that take?"

As he scratched his chin, Davy's eyes narrowed. "I could do a quick round, say in a couple of hours."

"Good."

Davy rose, towering above them much like the giant from *Jack and the Beanstalk*. "Help yourself to more soup if you want. I'll be back."

Jon stood and followed Davy to the door. He leaned close and whispered something.

"Yeah, I can, but it will cost you extra."

"I wouldn't expect less."

When Jon joined her at the table, she gave him a questioning look.

"You don't want to know, Lauren," he replied to her unvoiced question. She knew he was right.

"Lauren, sweetheart, wake up," Jon's voice called. She tried to shake off the intrusion into her sleep. "C'mon, love, wake up. I can't carry you to bed."

"I'll get her," a voice said.

Suddenly Lauren was swept up into strong arms and held against a large chest. Her eyes fluttered open. Davy grinned down at her.

"Go back to sleep, lass. Your old man is following us. I'm taking you to a more comfortable bed than my kitchen chair."

Lauren wanted to fight against the overwhelming drowsiness, but her body wouldn't cooperate.

"That's quite a head of hair your missus has," Davy said.

"Yeah, it is," Jon answered. There was pride in his voice that warmed her and made her smile as sleep overtook her.

Chapter 13

Voices pulled her from sleep.

"Did you discover anything?" Jon asked.

"I think I might have a bead on your man." Lauren recognized Davy's voice.

She opened her eyes and saw Davy and Jon huddled on the lumpy couch across the room.

"Go on," Jon urged.

"The name Parker James didn't mean anything to an associate of mine, but your description fit a man who's been going to him for the last four years." Davy rested his elbows on his knees. "It seems that this here gent got hisself in a bit of trouble with my friend. Couldn't pay off his losses on several races. Suddenly the bloke comes up with the money. Lots of money. 'Course, the mark continued to use my friend, and he's made 'im a rich man."

Lauren propped herself up on her elbows. If the man

they were discussing was Parker, then Parker certainly had good reason to be on the take.

Jon rubbed his chin. "Why is your friend so sure that this guy is Parker James?"

"Well, that's the interesting part. He had the gent followed. He wanted to be sure he got his money back. They discovered their sucker worked at the American embassy. You think we've got the right man?"

"Yeah, it sounds like it."

"There's another thing. This Parker James, he likes to dress up like a cowboy and strut his stuff for all the English ladies."

Jon's expression turned hard. "What? Has your man seen Parker dressed like that?"

"Sure, it's a big joke among the bookies that that cowboy wouldn't know one end of a horse from the other." Davy pointed toward Lauren. "It looks like your missus is awake. I'll go down and fix some tea."

Jon nodded absently. Davy rose and walked to the stairs.

"Davy," Jon called, stopping the other man. "Were you able to get me that item I asked for?"

He nodded. "It will be here before the end of the hour."

Lauren waited until she heard Davy downstairs before she asked, "What item, Jon?"

His gaze captured hers. "A gun, Lauren. I'm not going into this situation unarmed. Parker tried to kill me once, and he is probably the guy who killed Tony."

"How do you know that? I thought you said you didn't see the killer?"

"That's right. I didn't see his face before he knocked me out. But I did see his gray ostrich-skin cowboy boots."

His declaration stole the breath from her lungs. Parker a killer. The thought was almost incomprehensible. It was rather like watching the people she knew or thought she knew remove their masks and discovering the individual underneath was nothing like the outside disguise.

Jon sat beside her on the bed. "Lauren, I know this is hard for you, but it's something that has to be done. It appears that Parker's been selling our side out for money. Maybe if Parker believed the other side was right, I could understand—not approve—but understand his actions. But greed? He's slime beneath my feet."

The hardness in Jon's voice worried her. There would be no mercy for Parker. "Do you plan on killing him?"

"No, I don't plan to. What we want is his handler. And I'm sure Diamond would like to recover the radar system that was stolen. If Parker dies, then we're left with those loose ends." His hand cupped her cheek. "Don't worry, I won't kill him, although I'm tempted. I still know some right from wrong. I haven't been totally corrupted."

Tears clogged her throat. With trembling lips she brushed a kiss across his mouth. "It's still there inside you, Jonathan."

His brow furrowed in a frown. "What?"

"The heart of an idealist. The heart of a dreamer."

Jon waited in the kitchen for Lauren to finish her morning routine in the bathroom. What she said bothered him. He didn't have the heart of an idealist anymore. That had died long ago after the countless years of lying and being lied to. No, there was nothing left of that young man's soul.

And that's what worried him. If there was nothing left of the man he was, what did he have to offer Lauren to build a future upon?

Davy and Jon left Lauren in the kitchen to finish her toast and tea while they slipped into the pool room and did some business with a rather unsavory fellow.

Although Lauren was curious as to what they were doing in the other room, she decided it was best if she didn't know. Instead, she sipped her tea and browsed through the morning paper.

She was halfway through it when an article leaped out at her. Kitchen Fire At Local Restaurant Sends One To Hospital.

"No," she screamed, knocking over her mug of tea.

Instantly the men were in the kitchen.

"Lauren, what is it?" Jon asked, grabbing her by the shoulders.

She pointed to the news article. Jon snatched it up and read aloud.

"A kitchen fire at a local restaurant, Santa Fe Station, broke out last night around ten. There was one injury. The cook, Jimmy Mason, was taken to hospital. The fire marshal is still investigating the source of the fire."

"I need to find Jimmy," Lauren said. "Does it say which hospital?"

Jon reread the paragraph. "No."

"Then I'd better start calling. There are a lot of hospitals in this town."

* * *

Lauren rushed into Middlesex Hospital, not bothering to stop at the information desk since she already knew what room Jimmy was in from her phone call. Instead, she headed for the second floor. Jon trailed behind her.

Pushing open the door to Jimmy's room, Lauren came face-to-face with a nurse.

"May I help you?"

"I came to see Jimmy Mason."

Over the nurse's shoulder, Lauren could see Jimmy lying still as a corpse on the bed. His hair was singed, and there was a bandage around his head. Both his hands were wrapped in gauge. A clear mask covered Jimmy's nose and mouth.

The nurse eyed Lauren. "Because of the patient's condition. No visitors. Only family. Are you family?"

Jon's gaze met Lauren's. His brow rose, and he silently challenged her. What was she going to do? Lauren clearly remembered her lofty speech to Jon that lying was wrong. Now that she was backed into a corner, what was she going to do?

The temptation to lie was overwhelming, but if she was going to be able to face herself in the mirror, Lauren knew she couldn't. "He doesn't have any family. I'm the closest thing he has to one."

The woman didn't look convinced.

"Look, Jimmy needs to know he matters to someone. He matters to me."

"All right. But make it a short visit. He's not feeling too chipper this morning." The nurse looked at Jon. "You with her?"

"I'm her husband."

Lauren slowly approached the bed. A tenderness welled up inside her for the young Englishman, and she realized what she'd told the nurse was true. For her, Jimmy was family.

Lightly she brushed back strands of hair that tumbled over the bandage across his forehead. "Hello, you stubborn man." Warmth and affection colored her words.

Jimmy's eyes fluttered open. "Hi."

"How are you feeling?"

"Like I've been bashed in the head and thrown into hell."

Jon stepped to Lauren's side. "Do you recall what happened?" Jon asked Jimmy.

"Jon," Lauren rebuked. "This isn't the right time."

Jon looked at Jimmy, then at Lauren. "Yes, it is. If this was arson, we need to know. Was it, Jimmy?"

"Yeah. I ran late last night. I made up the bank deposit for the restaurant and intended to drop it off on my way to my flat. I turned off the light in the office and went into the kitchen. I heard a noise at the back door and went to investigate it. Next thing I knew, I woke up on the floor, fire all around me." He coughed, a deep hacking sound that indicated Jimmy had suffered from smoke inhalation.

"No more," she said. "I want you to rest."

Jimmy's eyes glistened with moisture. "I'm sorry about the restaurant."

She shook her head. "It wasn't your fault. Why would you even think that?" A tear rolled down her cheek.

"You loved that place."

"You are more important than any building."

Jon tugged at Lauren's arm. "We need to go."

She glanced over her shoulder at him. Jon had warned her that they could only spend a few minutes with Jimmy. He worried that the cops might come to question Jimmy, and they couldn't afford a run-in with the police. The second possibility that worried Jon was that the mole might be watching the hospital to try to set a trap for him and Lauren. She had promised before they had come to leave when he felt it was time. Now was the time.

Turning back to Jimmy, she smiled. "I'll be back to check on you." She leaned over and kissed his cheek. "Hurry and get well."

As they exited the room, Jon stopped her and pointed to the end of the hall by the elevator. There stood a uniformed policeman, talking to one of the nurses. Jon glanced around and pointed to the exit sign several doors down in the opposite direction.

Lauren hurried toward the stairs. As they descended the steps, she thought she heard Jon grumble, "Damn things."

Once they were outside, they raced toward the Escort.

"Where are you going?" Jon asked as she pulled out into traffic.

"I want to see the restaurant. After that, I'm all yours."

"I'll hold you to that promise."

Lauren stood on the sidewalk in front of the charred remains of her restaurant. Her expression was one of stunned disbelief.

"It can't be," she whispered, her gaze traveling over the burned-out building, as if looking a second time would change things. The fire had eaten everything but the outer walls.

She started into the building, but Jon grasped her arm, stopping her. "It's probably not safe, Lauren, to go inside. That's why they have tape around the place."

She looked up at him, and her eyes were nearly black with pain.

"We could walk around the place, if you like," he suggested, wanting to find some way to ease her anguish.

She nodded.

They slowly walked down the alley to peer into the blackened remains of the kitchen. "Five years of hard work are gone, vanished as if they never existed." Tears slipped down her cheeks.

Jon felt her pain as keenly as if it was his own. In a way it was. She was his, and if it touched her, it touched him. He transferred his cane from his right hand to his left, then wrapped his arm around her shoulders, pulling her to his side. "That's not true," he said, struggling to come up with the right words. "You learned so much in the past five years. It won't take you long to rebuild and get back into business. And your customers will return the instant you open."

"That might take some time." Parker's comment caused Lauren and Jon to turn toward the entrance to the alley. He held a gun in his hand, pointing it at them.

"Parker, what are you doing?" Lauren asked.

"I've come to get you and Greg. You see, Lauren, you've been hiding a fugitive. He killed his partner, Anthony Neil. Scotland Yard has been searching the country for him."

"And are you going to turn me over to them?" Jon asked.

Parker motioned with his gun. "C'mon. I've got someone who wants to talk to you."

Jon had allowed his arm to slip down behind Lauren. He was inching his hand toward the gun tucked in his belt in the middle of his back. His sport coat had hidden the fact he had a weapon. "Nice boots," Jon commented to Parker. "Gray ostrich, aren't they?"

The instant Parker glanced down, Jon stepped away from Lauren and went for his gun. He had it in his hand, but before he could fire, he was hit on the head. As the blackness swallowed him up, he heard Lauren's scream.

It seemed to happen all in slow motion. Jon stepping away from her, drawing his gun, the monster of a man coming up behind him and hitting Jon on the back of his head with the butt of a gun. Jon went down like a stone.

Lauren scrambled for the gun, but the giant grabbed her upper arm, hauled her to her feet and shook her like a toy.

"That's enough, Tiny," Parker commanded.

The giant released Lauren and stood over Jon.

"Go get the van and drive it into the alley. We'll load him in the back."

Tiny nodded and left. Lauren took a step toward Jon, but Parker waved her back with his gun.

"Move away from him, Lauren. I wouldn't want to hurt you." He stepped around Jon's body and picked up the gun. He glanced at it. "This isn't standard-issue CIA. I wonder where Greg got it." He slipped the gun into the front pocket of his suit coat.

"And are you CIA, too?" Lauren asked.

He smiled coldly.

"What's going on, Parker?"

"You'll find out soon enough." There was a puzzled expression on Parker's face. "I don't know what hold Greg Williams has over you, but you decided to hook up with the wrong man."

Greg Williams. Parker kept calling Jon "Greg Williams." Something wasn't fitting in this puzzle. Hadn't Jon insisted from the very beginning that the mole probably knew Jon was alive, and that was why he had come to warn her? And if Parker was the mole—and from the way he was waving the gun around, that seemed likely—then why did he insist on calling Jon by his cover name? Had Parker not made the connection? Or had Jon lied to her yet again?

"What do you mean?"

Parker's answer was forestalled by the arrival of a black panel van. The giant called Tiny drove it to where Jon lay, opened the back doors, then scooped him off the ground and placed him inside the van.

"Cuff him to the side," Parker ordered, handing Tiny the cuffs. After that was done, Parker motioned with the gun. "Lauren, you get in the front seat with Tiny and me." She started to reach down and retrieve Jon's cane, when Parker barked, "What are you doing?"

"Getting Greg's cane. I think he might need it when he wakes up." She held her breath, wondering if Parker knew the uniqueness of the cane. And even if he didn't, would it matter to him if Jon couldn't walk well without it?

"Okay."

She wrapped her fingers around the smooth wood and held it to her chest as she climbed into the van.

Parker followed her, sandwiching her between Tiny and himself.

"Where are you taking us?" she asked as they turned onto the street.

"I told you. To meet a friend."

She glanced over her shoulder, trying to see how Jon was faring. From all appearances, he was still unconscious.

"He's all right," Parker commented.

She wanted to ask Parker how *all right* he'd be if he was knocked in the head, but she wisely refrained. Lauren fought against the panic beating at her brain. She wasn't going to be any use to Jon or herself if she became hysterical. As she began to sort through her options, she realized that setting fire to her restaurant had been a ploy to draw her and Jon out into the open.

"You set the fire at Santa Fe Station, didn't you, Parker?"

"No, I can't say I did."

Her shoulders started to sag in relief until Tiny chuckled. It was a malicious sound that made her skin crawl.

"He didn't, but he hired the bugger who did."

At that moment Lauren knew they were hip deep in trouble.

The first thing that registered in Jon's foggy brain was the smell of the river, then the pounding of his head and the wrenching of his arm above his head. He lay still, eyes closed, and tried to sort out what had happened.

Parker. The gun. The blow from behind.

Where was Lauren? He opened one eye and saw Lauren seated between Parker and the driver.

"Go in the side entrance," Parker instructed.

Jon listened carefully to the sounds drifting into the van. Men shouted instructions for the unloading of a ship, accompanied by the harsh sound of a forklift. The water lapped against the hulls of the ships. The wharf.

Jon's mind raced. Why would Parker bring them here?

The van came to a halt, and he heard the three in the front seat get out. Next the back doors opened, and something tapped his foot.

"C'mon, Greg. Tiny didn't hit you that hard. Besides, I've got my gun in Lauren's side. You make any funny moves, and I'll shoot her. Tiny, unlock the cuffs."

Jon opened his eyes and stared at Parker's smirking face and Lauren's strained one. Jon didn't miss the fact that Parker kept calling him Greg. But that didn't make sense.

The van shifted under Tiny's weight, then the cuffs sprang open. Jon rolled his arms, trying to work out the kinks.

"Let's move," Parker commanded.

Jon slid to the back of the van and prepared to climb out.

"Here," Lauren said, thrusting his cane at him. There was some message in her eyes, but he couldn't figure out what it was. Parker's hand shot out, grasped Lauren's arm and pulled her back, away from him. Jon fought the urge to smash Parker over the head with his cane. The only thing that stopped him was the gun Tiny held on him.

Bracing the cane on the ground, he eased his feet onto the pavement.

Parker tugged Lauren toward the warehouse. Jon followed, with Tiny trailing behind. There were voices at the rear of the building from men unloading something. Maybe if he created a stir, the workers would come to investigate it.

"You make any noise and she'll be the first to die," Parker told Jon, stepping aside to allow Jon to see the gun nestled against Lauren's back. Parker didn't know it, Jon thought, but he had just signed his own death warrant.

Parker nudged Lauren toward a set of steel stairs in the corner. Lauren glanced over her shoulder, and her gaze met Jon's. Although there was fear in her green eyes, they also reflected her confidence in him.

The noise from the back of the warehouse drowned out their noisy ascent up the steel steps. There were several offices on the second level. Parker motioned Lauren to the last office at the end of the hall.

The door was open, and Lauren gasped when she entered the room. Jon was a step behind her.

"Hello, my dear," Marshall Blake greeted her, a deadly smile on his face. He was seated behind the large wooden desk. "Ah, I see you caught both fish, Parker. It's about time you did something right."

Parker's body tightened with the insult. So there was a rift between the coconspirators, Jon mused. Maybe he could use it to his and Lauren's advantage.

"Tiny," Marshall said, "go down to the fish warehouse and fetch me two barrels. Bring them back here."

The large man nodded and left the room, closing the door behind him. Marshall stood and moved around the desk. "Have a seat," he commanded, pointing at the chairs set before the desk.

Lauren looked at Jon, and he nodded for her to follow Marshall's order.

"Very smart of you, Greg. Your cooperation will make things easier."

"Oh, how will it help?" Jon asked, his fingers clutching his cane. "You'll kill us quickly?"

"You're dead, but I might be persuaded to spare Lauren. Several of my clients would pay handsomely for a woman like her."

Jon fought the rage that Marshall wanted to provoke in him. Rage wouldn't save Lauren from this hell. A cool, level head would.

Marshall folded his arms across his chest. "So, did you figure out how our little spy ring works? I believe you and Tony named it ROSES. I rather fancy that name. I think I'll keep it after you've been disposed of." He glanced from Jon to Lauren. "It really wasn't such a difficult puzzle. I'm almost surprised at how long it took you to figure it out.... So, what or who finally helped you connect the dots?"

Thankfully Lauren remained quiet, and Jon knew she was allowing him to take the lead.

"Nothing to say?" Marshall asked.

"I see no reason to allow you the opportunity to know your weak points," Jon answered. "I'll leave you to wonder where they are."

Marshall lunged at Lauren. He grasped her arm, lifting her out of the chair, and yanked it up behind her back. She tried to swallow her moan but wasn't successful. Jon started to rise, but Marshall tugged on her arm again. Jon slumped back into the chair.

"Now are you going to answer my question? Was it Lauren seeing my shopping list that tipped you off?"

"Yes, that was it."

Marshall released Lauren's arm, and she slumped in her chair. "You see, Parker," Marshall said as he settled back against the desk, "I was right to keep an eye on her. Did you like the little accidents I arranged for you, Lauren?"

Jon saw in her eyes the realization that he'd been right. "I can't say that I did," she quietly answered.

Laughter erupted from Marshall's chest. He rubbed his chin. "My question is, what brought you two together?" He gazed at Jon. "What was it? Did she go to you with the information?"

The question flashed brightly in his mind, and at that moment Jon realized that Marshall and Parker didn't have a clue to his real identity. Either he'd been betrayed by Diamond, or his boss had been fed a lie.

Marshall kicked Jon's knee. "I asked you a question. Answer it."

"I went looking for Parker one day to ask him about the list, only he wasn't around so I mentioned the list to Tony," Lauren quickly interjected, sitting at the edge of her chair. "Greg came to me with questions after Tony's death."

"I was afraid of that. It was sloppy of me to leave that list in the book, but how was I to know you'd discover it?"

Her eyes widened. "You were there in the library?"

"Watching your every move."

Jon wanted to divert Marshall from his questioning of Lauren. She'd done a good job keeping her cool, but he didn't want to put more strain on her than necessary.

"Who are you selling the radar system to?"

Marshall's attention moved back to Jon. "Interested, huh?" He looked at Parker, hovering over Lauren. "You think I should tell him?"

"No," Parker answered.

"But a dying man's last wish should be granted."
Marshall straightened. "I think you'll appreciate how
cleverly we've packed the system to ship to our client.
Let's go downstairs and look."

"But the workers?" Parker protested.

"Don't worry. They are paid well not to notice
things."

They walked downstairs, and Marshall threaded his
way through the stacked crates to the deserted front
corner of the warehouse. Emerging suddenly into a
small open space, completely isolated from the rest of
the warehouse by big crates, Marshall stopped dead
when he saw Donald bent over a case in the corner labeled Caviar. Donald straightened and held out what
looked like a computer chip.

"Why is this packed in this caviar crate?" he asked
his father.

"It's nothing to concern you, son."

Donald glanced over Marshall's shoulder and stiffened when he saw Lauren. "What's she doing here?"

Jon watched Parker move behind Lauren. Although
the gun Parker held wasn't visible, Jon knew it was
pressed against Lauren.

"What are *you* doing here?" Marshall asked his son,
ignoring the question asked of him.

Donald pointed to the crate. "I promised Mr. Kowalski a box of caviar. I was hoping to undo the dam-
age my ex-fiancée did the other night."

"Leave his address with my secretary, and it will be
sent out this afternoon."

A look of rebellion crossed Donald's face.

"Goodbye," Marshall said.

Donald started toward the door, then stopped when
he was beside Lauren.

"Donald, I'd like to talk to you," Lauren said, latching onto his arm. "Could we go somewhere private?"

After a moment of indecision, he nodded. "All right." Donald looked at Parker. "Care to release the lady's arm?"

"Son, this isn't the time for a chat."

Donald glared at Parker, then tugged at Lauren's other arm. Parker didn't let go.

Jon knew what Lauren was doing. She was preparing to use one of her self-defense moves that she had employed against him. And while he silently cursed her pigheadedness, he prepared himself to move when she did.

Lauren stomped on Parker's instep, then dropped to the floor, breaking free of both men's grips. Jon rammed into Donald's back, shoving him into several crates and away from Lauren. Grabbing his cane by the shaft, he wielded it like a club and hit Parker's wrist, causing the hand to go numb. The gun fell to the floor.

Parker lunged for the gun. Jon struck him again with his cane at the point where his shoulder met his neck. Parker crumpled to the floor unconscious.

"Behind you, Jon," Lauren screamed. He whirled, arms raised, and was able to intercept the small crate Marshall had aimed at his head. Jon staggered back from the blow and fell over Donald's body.

Marshall ducked behind a large crate and then suddenly appeared with the gun in his hand. He grabbed Lauren by the hair.

"Get up," he growled, the gun aimed at her head.

Marshall kept Jon in his sight while she struggled to stand. The instant she was on her feet, Marshall grabbed her around the neck and pressed the gun to her temple.

"Now we're going to try this all over again. Donald, get out of here."

The younger Blake staggered up and looked at Lauren, then his dad. He didn't question anything, but simply turned toward the door and left.

Sniveling worm, Jon thought. *How could Lauren have almost married such an unprincipled coward?*

Marshall kicked Parker in the leg. "Wake up."

Parker moaned.

Marshall kicked him again. "Get up."

Parker's eyes fluttered open.

"Get on your feet or I'm going to shoot you where you lie."

Parker rolled to his knees and, using several crates, pulled himself upright.

Marshall looked at Jon. "She called you Jon. Would that be Jonathan Michaels?"

Jon didn't respond.

"Well, it certainly makes sense why Lauren went to you."

"She didn't know," Jon replied.

Marshall shrugged. "We weren't sure about your death the last time. That's why we decided to let Parker keep an eye on Lauren. It doesn't matter. You're going to die this time."

Jon took a step forward. "You don't have to hurt Lauren. She's the innocent one in all this."

"She knows too much. But I will miss her. I looked forward to having her as a daughter-in-law." He nodded toward the corner. "Parker, there is rope and some rags over there. Get them and tie these two up until I can arrange to dispose of their bodies."

Parker retrieved the rope and tied Lauren's and Jon's hands behind their backs, roped them together back-to-back at the shoulders, waists, and legs, then stuffed foul-smelling rags into their mouths. Marshall and Parker dragged them behind the crate bearing the radar system and laid them on the floor.

"Tie their feet to the screw hook in the side beam," Marshall instructed. Parker anchored their feet to the hook.

Marshall bent over the prone couple on the floor. "Enjoy your last hour."

Jon's mind raced, trying to figure out a way to get them out of this mess. He didn't know how much time they had, but he didn't think it would take Marshall long to arrange their deaths.

"Will," Marshall's voice rang out in the back of the warehouse. "Have your crew take a lunch break."

"It's only eleven, sir."

"Do it."

Jon's fingers sought out Lauren's. He tried to untie her hands, but his fingers seemed too clumsy. After several attempts, Lauren grasped his hands, stilling them. She wiggled her body. Jon didn't understand what she was doing, but hoped she had an idea on how to get them out of this mess.

She wiggled again, the motion reminding him of an eel. Suddenly he felt something hard slide under his hip. His cane. Straining, he grabbed the cane and put the head in Lauren's hands. He then twisted the shaft, separating the blade from the wood.

His fingers worked the shaft down until he freed the knife. He took the weapon from her and began to saw through the ropes. After several frustrating minutes and several unpleasant pokes from the knife tip, he was successful in cutting away the rope from his hands. He worked his arms around his body, then slipped them out from under the rope at their waists. Then he reached back, grabbed his knife and quickly cut the remaining ropes. They spit out the gags.

Marshall's and Parker's voices rang out in the quiet building. They were coming back. Jon and Lauren got to their feet and moved along the wall toward the door.

"I want you to help Tiny get them into the barrels," Marshall said. "We'll dump them in the channel. No one will ever recover their bodies."

Jon chanced a glance at the corner where they had been tied. Marshall and Blake stood staring at the cut ropes on the floor. Both held guns with silencers.

"Dammit, they've escaped," Marshall roared. "You stupid bastard, can't you do anything right?"

Jon crouched down and urged Lauren toward the door. They had almost made it when his bad knee gave out and he tumbled into several boxes.

"There," Marshall yelled, "by the door."

"Go," Jon commanded Lauren.

Things seemed to happen at once. Marshall's gun went off. Lauren staggered and fell. Then the side door flew open and half a dozen armed men spilled into the building. From the back of the warehouse, shouts filled the air, and then more men surged into the warehouse behind Marshall and Parker.

Jon peered up at the man closest to him. Diamond stood above him.

"Gentlemen," Diamond addressed Marshall and Parker. "We can have a shoot-out if you want, but you'll lose. So I would advise you to put down your weapons."

Parker carefully set his gun on the floor. Marshall glared at his cohort and then at Diamond.

Diamond smiled. "Please shoot. I want an excuse to fill you full of holes."

The threat had its intended effect, and Marshall laid down his weapon. Instantly both men were surrounded by agents. Jon ignored the activity. His attention was focused on where Lauren went down. Hurrying to her side, he found her lying on the floor, blood flowing down her face.

"Get help," Jon yelled, kneeling beside her. He pushed back her hair, trying to spot where she had been wounded. Instantly his hand was covered with her blood. The bullet had creased the side of her head. He pulled off his shirt and held it to the bleeding wound.

"How is she?" Diamond asked, squatting by Lauren.

Jon's burning gaze locked with his boss's. "Why would you care, you sorry bastard?"

Diamond sighed. "You found out."

"Yeah, I did. You've got my resignation."

"Jon—"

"Save it for someone who's interested."

The blare of an ambulance siren filled the air. Several seconds later two attendants rushed in and took Lauren from Jon's arms.

"How is she?" Jon asked the paramedics.

"It appears to be a flesh wound."

"I want to go with her. I'm her husband."

The men nodded and wheeled Lauren to the ambulance.

"Jon," Diamond called out.

Jon climbed into the back of the ambulance and looked at his boss.

"I had a reason for what I did."

"I know you did. But it doesn't change the fact I won't ever trust you again, and I'll never work for you again in this lifetime."

Lauren woke to the wailing siren of the ambulance. The pulsing noise only added to her throbbing headache.

"How are you feeling, *lieveling?*" Jon's smile was unsteady as he gazed down at her.

"Like I've been kicked in the head by my Aunt Milly's mule."

He took her hand in his and brought it up to his lips for a tender kiss. "I thought I'd lost you." His aching tone touched Lauren's heart. "I can only imagine what you went through when you heard I was dead. Forgive me, love."

His eyes, filled with naked pain, showed her the condition of his heart. There was no lie here.

"I think I understand why you didn't let me know you were alive after seeing the evil side of Marshall and Parker. They covered their true selves well."

"Don't worry, they'll die in jail, so they won't have the chance to fool another innocent."

"They didn't know, did they?"

"We'll talk about it later."

The edges of her vision were beginning to blur again. "Jon." Panic clutched her heart.

"It's okay, Lauren, I'm here. And I won't leave you ever again."

They were comforting words that eased her into the darkness.

* * *

Jon held Lauren's hand, waiting for her to wake. The worst moment of his life was when he saw Lauren fall after Marshall had discharged his gun. If Marshall wasn't hidden away in some interrogation room with CIA and probably MI6 men grilling him, Jon would've gone after him with the intent to kill.

After the events of this morning, Jon now understood Lauren's perspective on his lying. Diamond's betrayal left a bitter taste in his mouth, and he didn't know if he could ever forgive his old friend.

There was another truth that had been revealed to him today. Lauren had been right—at least partially. He had clung to very idealistic notions about honesty and faithfulness. Now those few beliefs were dead.

"How's she doing?" Diamond asked from the doorway to the room.

"They say she's going to be okay."

"Jon, we need to talk."

"Go ahead, but I doubt there's anything you can say that will absolve you."

"The pope's in that business. I'm not."

Jon slowly stood. "No, you're in the business of deception and dishonesty. And they couldn't have picked a better man for the job."

The muscles in Diamond's jaw flexed. "You're right. I'm good at what I do. I had hoped you would never find out how good."

"Why did you do it?" Jon desperately needed to know the answer.

"Well, it all seemed to hit the fan at the same time. I had several crises mishandled, then some little snot-nosed committee staffer of a senator came across the thefts from NATO. After the third one, I had three senators, the National Security Agency, and the president all breathing down my neck, wanting answers. I thought the quickest way to flush the mole was to tell you that you'd been made. I knew you'd warn Lauren, and I thought that might bring the mole out looking for you."

"Was there a break-in?"

"Yes."

"Then why didn't you plant my fingerprints there so Parker *would* know I was around?"

Diamond walked to the window and stared out. "Because, Jon, I discovered I couldn't throw you to the wolves." He turned to Jon. "How long have I been in this business? Twenty-five years, and I couldn't bring myself to hang you out to dry, no matter how beneficial it would've been. I wouldn't have been able to sleep at night." Shrugging, he added, "It's as simple as that. When you were in Glasgow and told me you were coming back to London, I knew I needed to be here, because all hell was going to cut loose. I was with you, Jon, the entire way."

"But you waited until Marshall and Blake made their move. You may have regretted what you did, but you used it."

"Hell, yes. After all you'd been through, I couldn't see throwing that away over a little guilt."

"He deserves to be forgiven," Lauren whispered into the quiet room.

Jon rushed to the bed. "You're awake."

"Obviously. There are two guys in my room arguing loudly."

Diamond stepped close. "It's good to see you awake, Lauren. I've heard a great deal about you."

She raised her brow, then winced at the pain the movement caused. "So, you're the infamous Diamond. I don't think I like you."

The stunned expression on his face made her smile. He returned the grin.

"I now see what attracted Jon to you."

"A sharp tongue?"

"A sharp mind. I'm sorry you had to be involved in this mess."

"Sometimes we don't have a choice." As she repeated the words Jon had said to her in Jimmy's apartment, she turned to him. "Sometimes when we do, it's a choice between bad and worse." Her hand reached for Jon's. "I understand."

Diamond cleared his throat. "If you'll excuse me, I have a plane to catch."

"Tell him now," Lauren said to Jon.

Jon didn't have to be told what Lauren was referring to. He knew. She wanted him to forgive Diamond. But he couldn't do it at this point.

"I understand," Jon murmured.

Both men knew the breach still lay between them. But Jon understood the reasoning behind Diamond's actions.

Diamond nodded. "I have something for you, Jon." From his inside suit-coat pocket he withdrew an envelope and set it on the hospital tray table. "Goodbye. I'll contact you soon." Without a backward glance, he left the room.

Lauren eyed his hospital jacket. "You look very natty."

He glanced down at his white lab coat. "My shirt was covered with blood. The nurses lent me this."

"Oh. How's Jimmy?" she asked.

"He's doing fine. He should be released tomorrow. He was asking about you."

"I'm glad he's recovered." Her eyes darkened. "What happened to Donald?"

"He's being held as an accessory to kidnapping and attempted murder. We don't think he knew about his father's spying, but when he walked out of that warehouse, leaving you to be killed, he committed a crime."

Jon stroked his fingers over her cheek. "Can you forgive me, Lauren, for lying to you? I swear to you I may not have leveled with you about my job, but I never lied about my feelings for you."

"After living your life for the last few days, I have a new appreciation of your job. I can't throw any stones."

He leaned down and tenderly kissed her, then drew back.

"What did your boss leave?" Lauren asked, pointing to the envelope.

Jon retrieved it and brought it to the bed. He ripped the end off and shook it. Into his palm fell a thin gold wedding ring.

"Is it . . . ?" Her voice trailed off.

Jon picked up the ring and read aloud the inscription on the inside. "To Jon, Love Lauren." His fingers closed around it. "I thought I lost it in the accident. He had it all this time."

"Maybe he didn't think you were ready to have it back."

Maybe he hadn't, Jon admitted. Maybe he hadn't been ready to come back to Lauren before. But now he was. Now he was prepared to give her every part of himself, leaving nothing in the shadows. But the choice was hers.

Jon placed the ring in Lauren's hand. "It's yours. Do with it what you wish."

She fingered the band, then reached for his left hand and slipped it on his ring finger. "That's where it belongs."

Seeing the love shining in her eyes, Jon knew that her love offered him a new start with new hopes and new dreams. "Do you mean that?" he asked.

"Yes."

He tenderly gathered her into his arms. "I don't know what I'm going to do, Lauren. But I don't think I can continue to live in the shadows."

"I'm going to need help rebuilding my restaurant and I think I'd like a collaborator on my book. I can't think of anyone better to help me plot murder and mayhem. You think you might like to take the job?"

"For the rest of my life."

She peered up at him. "I'll keep you to that promise."

He brushed a kiss across her lips. "I love you, Lauren. I have since the first moment I set eyes upon you."

"And I love you. I never stopped. And I never will."

A soft peace settled around his heart. He pulled her against his chest. "For that miracle, I'll thank heaven every day."

* * * * *

COMING NEXT MONTH

**The wedding celebration was so nice...
too bad the bride wasn't there!**

*Runaway
Brides*

Find out what happens when three brides have a
change of heart.

Three complete stories by some of your favorite
authors—all in one special collection!

YESTERDAY ONCE MORE
by Debbie Macomber

FULL CIRCLE
by Paula Detmer Riggs

THAT'S WHAT FRIENDS ARE FOR
by Annette Broadrick

Available this June wherever books are sold.

Look us up on-line at:http://www.romance.net

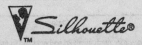

Silhouette's recipe for a sizzling summer:

* Take the best-looking cowboy in South Dakota
* Mix in a brilliant bachelor
* Add a sexy, mysterious sheikh
* Combine their stories into one collection and you've got one sensational super-hot read!

Summer Sizzlers
MEN OF Summer

Three short stories by these favorite authors:

Kathleen Eagle
Joan Hohl
Barbara Faith

Available this July wherever
Silhouette books are sold.

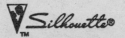

SS96

You're About to Become a Privileged Woman

Reap the rewards of fabulous free gifts and benefits with proofs-of-purchase from Silhouette and Harlequin books

Pages & Privileges™

It's our way of thanking you for buying our books at your favorite retail stores.

PROOF OF PURCHASE
SIM-PP148
Offer expires October 31, 1996

Pages & Privileges ™

Harlequin and Silhouette—
the most privileged readers in the world!

For more information about Harlequin and Silhouette's PAGES & PRIVILEGES program call the Pages & Privileges Benefits Desk: 1-503-794-2499

Silhouette®

SIM-PP148